W............R

for Jane

SARAH CONNELL

with much love
Sarah H

Cinnamon Press
:: small miracles from distinctive voices ::

Published by Cinnamon Press
Meirion House
Tanygrisiau
Blaenau Ffestiniog
Gwynedd LL41 3SU
www.cinnamonpress.com

The right of Sarah Connell to be identified as author of this work has been asserted by her in accordance with the Copyright, Designs and Patent Act, 1988. © 2019 Sarah Connell. ISBN 978-1-78864-047-3

Designed and typeset in Garamond by Cinnamon Press. Cover design: Adam Craig © Adam Craig. Cover image: Sean King/Unsplash.

Cinnamon Press is represented by Inpress and by the Welsh Books Council in Wales. Printed in Poland.

The publisher acknowledges the support of the Welsh Books Council.

Acknowledgements

With warm thanks to Rowan Fortune.

Whenever

Chapter One

It starts with a phone call in the night. She comes out of a heavy sleep with a judder; that night harbinger of disaster is ringing. She rolls, registering as she does so that the other side of the bed is empty. Lifting the receiver with one hand, she stretches the other behind her in an awkward movement. The sheet is cold.

It starts with a phone call in the night. Only silence while she listens. A strange quality of silence as if someone is mouthing words, straining to speak but sounding nothing.

Fear enters her, squeezing her chest. For a second, the familiar shapes in the dark room are blurred and strange. Where is he? She checks the time. The digital display blinks. Exactly four o'clock. The middle of the night. Ray is a careful man, a considerate husband. He has not rung to say he would be late. Where could he be? Who was it that has rung and said nothing?

The arrangement to see his friend, Martin, in the pub is occasional, confirmed by a phone call the night before. 'Yes, fine, eight is fine for me.' His deep voice in the hall. And he had left yesterday evening in time to walk to the centre, a ten minute stroll to the town's quiet bar, avoiding the hectic bands of drinkers on the main street. Could she ring his friend, at this time, to see, to confirm, that he stayed over at his house for some reason, that he is sleeping there? He would ring himself. He would never leave her worried, awake in the dark and frightened for him. For her. When it was time for her alarm at 7.15 he would ring. His face, a heavy oval, serious, crumpled by time at the edges. How long since she has touched his face? She shuts her eyes and lays down. She must wait for morning, but she will not be able to sleep.

The second awakening is worse because her mind knows before she is conscious that he is not here. Somehow she has slept and her alarm radio tells her about wars and far-off dramas, but Ray has not rung.

Something bad has happened. Maybe he is ashamed of getting drunk, staying out. Maybe he will turn up soon.

Ray is rarely drunk. He moderates himself. He is careful, restrained. Her body stiffens, her limbs rigid.

Her uniform is hanging in the bathroom, waiting, clean, white, trimmed blue. How she loves her uniform. Training, dedication, a new life in her forties and a useful role, helping so many. Using touch and movement to heal, console, bring about recovery. She straightens the bedclothes on her side as habit demands, putting the decorative cushions back. But where she has pushed the duvet down on his side, searching for his warmth, she leaves it. An untidy room, a disturbed bed. An empty space.

Instead of a shower and quickly dressing for work at the hospital, she meanders through the house, listening, waiting, into the kitchen. The kitchen has white tiles and cupboards, with touches of blue from her display of china on one shelf, carefully placed and frequently washed items she had chosen to fit this kitchen, this picture. Ray professed indifference to the colour scheme, but congratulated her when it was finished. She is proud of its clean simplicity; it is tasteful and hygienic.

Without knowing what she is doing, she pours her usual cereal into a bowl. She looks at it as if it is alien. She sits at the table, lifts the spoon to her mouth. Then slowly drops it. A few splashes fall silently onto the table. She gets up, takes a cloth from its place next to the sink and wipes the milky marks. She rinses the cloth, hangs it back and sits again. The cereal waits uneaten.

Outside soft autumnal rain falls, before the forecast storms. The acer and the cherry tree in the garden are still in full green leaf, but the first signs of change have begun, gold and bronze flashes in the branches. Christine planted them in their first summer. She loves the vivid red of the acer when it turns in late autumn and anticipates its glory with pleasure every year. The old magnolia, which was here when they bought the house ten years ago, is the last to change, its heavy leaves only going brown and dropping later in the season. Still sitting, facing the window, she waits. For a phone call, a message, for something to happen.

On the side of the bread bin, she sees his phone. He has not taken his phone. Something bad has happened.

She forces herself to open his side of the wardrobe cupboards. Empty hangers reproach her, only his two suits and some old trousers still hang, left behind.

Later in the morning, she decides she must ring the hospital to explain she is not coming in for her shift. She will have to say she is unwell. She wonders how to phrase this. Her sickness record is unbroken, remarked on by all her managers over seven years. As she still sits, staring out of the window, practising what she might say, the house phone rings. She springs to her feet and runs up the hall. But as she reaches it —is she going too slowly, is she unable to run quickly enough —the answer service starts.

She stands in front of the machine and listens intensely.

'Hi Ray, just a quick one, sorry you couldn't make it last night, but I am free this pm and would like to see you, old boy. Let me know. Off to work now but my mobile, you know?'

Martin does not know where Ray is. They did not meet last night. He will ring again. She will tell him Ray has left her. He will come solicitiously, expressing concern. But he and she are not friends. His embarrassment will keep him away after that visit. His embarrassment and her unspoken shame.

What could have happened to him? She must ring the hospital, the police, someone.

The refrain, 'something bad has happened,' runs through her mind. She mouths it as she wanders through the house. It is a charm, a chant against the absence of her steady, faithful husband, the academic one, who could be trusted to do the decent thing, the expected action.

She stands in front of a mirror in the bedroom. She sees a small blonde person she cannot recognise. Her eyes cloud with something other than tears.

In the afternoon, she rings the police. Speaking clearly and slowly, her heart pounding, she says she has a missing person to report. Three officers arrive, solemn, respectful, taking notes, sitting on her and Ray's sofas in their uniforms, apparently untroubled.

'Have there been any trouble marital problems between you?'

'Do you know of any difficulties he may have been having?'

'Do you know if he has been going to work regularly?'

'Has he been to work this week?'

She realises she has not wondered about work. She doesn't know if he is at work at this moment. While she is facing police officers in her home, could he be teaching, sitting at a desk, only a short walk away? She tenses her legs as if to spring up to go and see.

Has he been to work? The senior one takes his time to talk it through with her, leading her inexorably, sentence by carefully spaced sentence, to the point where it could be said, in a thoughtful voice with steady eyes gazing into hers, that 'there was no real risk involved.' His companions nod thoughtfully in agreement. A man of fifty three, no obvious health problems, no mental health record. He will be registered on the system as a missing person. But, in fact, he is free. Free to go. Free to leave as he wishes. Unless she has anything else to add.

He has just left. Left the car, his phone and some clothes as well as her.

'Doesn't it mean?', she asks, her voice rising, 'Isn't it, isn't it a risk that he has not rung me or left any, any sign?'

Surely he is a missing person who must be looked for? Their eyes are sympathetic, but the negative hangs between them.

The female officer says she will be her contact, gives her a card with a name and number, to keep and use if there is any news. This official, with a cool look of professional sympathy, is her only link with the search. If there is a search.

She imagines helicopters in the sky whirring above woodland, dogs straining to follow scents, masses of officers combing inches of grass for clues. Is he to vanish without an outcry?

The advice leaflet the police leave, a leaflet for people like her who have inexplicably lost someone, has words she can read, but not follow.

Their joint account is untouched, but he has his own money. His wallet is gone. After two days she goes through his drawers; not all of his clothes have gone. He had left that evening, seventy two hours earlier, and called out goodbye. She was watching television, did not turn, did not see if he was carrying a bag. Had he been careful to leave when she was occupied? She puts her hands onto what is left of the folded underwear and sweaters, soft and bulky, like himself. She smoothes their surfaces, looking at her hands, the broad capable hands she has always known. Hands she uses for her work. Hands he has slipped through. She laughs. What an idea for a wife; 'he slipped through my fingers!' Shaken by laughter, she sits on the bed on his side. The laughter turns to hot tears. She weeps furiously for long moments. How dare he be free.

Chapter Two

When she rings the following morning, the female officer explains that there has been no sign of him. He has not been recorded on CCTV in town; there have been no sightings. Her voice is professional, detached and cool. Perhaps she is a specialist dealing with missing persons. Then the officer suggests Christine contacts his work. The call is over.

She rings the College where he is a lecturer in maths and geography. She is put through to the staff room as she knew she would be. She cannot say who she is. You cannot say you do not know where your husband is. At the last second, as the staff voice answers, she thinks of a name to call herself, a name she remembers Ray mentioning, an adult student who has been a nuisance, always demanding more help, more time from him.

'Can I speak to Ray Armitage. It's Shirley.' She has to hope the person on the other end will not recognise her voice or know Shirley's.

She doesn't know the voice she is listening to but she hears the hesitation and confused assessment.

'Ray is on sabbatical this year. Perhaps you didn't know. Sorry I can't give him a message as we have only seen him to say goodbye. Can anyone else help?'

She drops the phone on its stand. Confirmation of his desertion of his post as her husband, of his care for her. Leaving without a word, except to others. Leaving with a plan, made in advance, talked to his department about a plan he had written letters about. She sits. Her breathing is harsh and the room swims. He has arranged an exit, one she knows takes time and effort and agreement. How could he talk to his Head of Department, fatherly Malcolm, about a sabbatical year, and not tell her? Where has he gone and why? Why has he planned to hurt her? What has she done?

She can hear the boys at their morning games in the playing fields behind their row of houses. Usually she would be at work. She stands in the white gleam of the kitchen, looking out. The noises, sometimes whistles and then shouts, rise and fall. When they first saw this house, the proximity of the school was a problem. Especially to Ray.

'We don't want to listen to kids all day.'

Later, 'The parents might be a nuisance too, those private school types.'

But the main gate, where the children arrive and parents drive up in their huge vehicles, is around the corner. The only land close to their garden is the sports field stretching behind their road. Sometimes in the summer you can hear cricket practice in the long, light evenings. Or there might be a summer athletics event on a Saturday.

Today she stands, rooted, and listens to young voices pitched into the air, the booming of teachers; 'Come on, Smithson, move yourself, that's it, Weller, well done.'

A pain goes through her chest. A different pain. They can't see her, she can't see them. I am an invisible woman. The childless woman with no husband. The woman no one knows.

She realises she did not ask where the sabbatical was. That must mean the staff in his Department at the College all know where he has gone. Why didn't the police tell her? Have they not even investigated what his Head of Department, Malcolm, knows? She cannot remember if the officer said they had spoken to him. She goes into the hall and stands by the phone. She must ring the College again.

The phone rings. 'Don't.' she screams silently. 'Don't ring me. I am a marked woman. invisible, nobody, a stranger.'

But she must answer it. Calmly she lifts the phone. It is Gillian.

She starts to speak but can only make dry, sobbing noises, sobs forced out of her chest. 'Chrissie, I am on my way.'

Gillian is there twenty minutes later. Holding out her arms, taking Christine into a hug. But she cannot let go, cannot relax into this offer of tears on the shoulder. She is stiff and pushes away. How can she explain to this steady person with a predictable, safe life that her husband has cleared off by choice. Christine is no longer safe.

There is an unpolished look about Gillian, her clothes a little lumpy, the faintest bristle of a moustache if you look. Her mouth is made for disapproval even when expressing sympathy. The kindness of strangers. Gillian is no stranger though, an old friend, once a neighbour.

Gillian is someone you can rely on to care, to pay attention, to be there in a crisis. She is doing that, but Christine cannot be cared for. Please go away, she wants to say. Leave me. I am someone who has been left.

Gillian bustles around, making tea, writing a list, a list of what she does not know, talking and then sitting and asking her to talk. Christine is dry mouthed and cannot speak.

Gillian shakes her head when she has forced a few words out.

'Gone? What do you mean, he has just gone? Is he a missing person? Officially I mean. What do the police say? How could he do this to you? Are you sure there is no note anywhere?'

She cannot tell Gillian about the sabbatical year. This betrayal is a secret held even closer.

'Look, come to our house. Stay with us.'

The idea of being with Gillian and her stuffy, slow-wit of a husband, as Ray has always called Eddie, is unthinkable.

'Oh, my dear. Be brave. I will phone every day. Just let me know if anything happens and I will come round whenever you want. You know that, don't you?'

She does know that.

As Gillian is leaving she says 'Ray is a rat. Sorry, Chrissie, but this is unforgivable.'

How does Gillian know what can be forgiven? How does anyone know?

When the daily phone calls come, she wants to shout, 'Don't ring me, don't talk your endless comforting nonsense, stay away from me.'

But controlling her breath, she has an answer. 'No news, Gillian. I am okay. Really I am. As okay as I can be. Please don't worry about me.'

In the bedroom, she stands in front of the mirror and looks: a neat body she had always been proud of, small boned but strong, with fair hair that behaves itself tied back or hanging to her shoulders, a face where she can see lines forming from her nose and across her forehead. She has a flat stomach. She is forty seven and childless. Now husbandless too, she thinks. At night the house talks to itself, a slow dialogue that keeps her anxiously awake. Each creak or knock might be a declaration of his return. A pain lodges itself in her chest as she lies down.

After a week, she goes back to work. She will not tell her colleagues she has lost a husband. She walks slowly round the corner of the street, turns left and walks up the slope of North Avenue towards the hospital. Wind has brought bright coppers onto the pavement at the corner, shining beech leaves at her feet. Up the hill, she passes the mulberry tree which has left purple stains from its ungathered fruit. Myth has it that there was one of these trees in the city's prison yard, the origin of the children's song, going around the tree the only exercise the inmates had. She turns along the cinder track. Ahead of her, thin jogging bottoms cling in the breeze to the calves of a woman walking in the same direction, her body a miracle of fat padding, each limb swollen beyond its natural shape. Chrissie slows down further, wanting to avoid a conversation or to pass rudely without speaking.

The turquoise and yellow panels of the new buildings shine as she crosses by the side of the car park, head down. As she nears the grand atrium entrance she lifts her eyes and composes her face. She walks around the building to the Out Patients entrance. Her colleague, Paveen, rushes through Physiotherapy Reception to greet her. She is a short, round-faced woman, a young colleague who shares gossip with a wicked grin, gives out youtube recommendations, bustles with warmth and quiet energy. Christine looks away from her dark eyes and manages to field her concerned enquiries.

'I am fine now. Yes, really'

'Well, thank goodness you are back. It's been hell and more!' Paveen says

Christine gives a grimace of assumed sympathy, apologising again about the patient list she has missed. Luckily they are as busy as usual, and she has a full list of appointments to be seen in the outpatients clinic. Later she goes to do her rounds on the wards.

She has to put a young girl, who is recovering from surgery, through painful but necessary exercises. It takes all her concentration to support the child, to encourage, to use her touch to reassure. The necessity of her professional poise is a relief.

At night she dreams of a landscape that they are both walking through. It is familiar, yet unknown, a pattern of fields above cliffs she cannot identify. He is ahead, briskly pacing a narrow path. She reaches out, stretches her arms to hold him back. But he presses on. She is confused as sleep painfully recedes. Had she felt irritation or love in the dream? In life she is always ahead on their walks, always going faster, annoying him with her speed, her longing to go on, to feel wind and space.

Another night she dreams of a baby crying somewhere far away in a room she cannot reach, however much she struggles to find it. The old dream. It has returned when she thought, after years, she has found acceptance and peace. She sits in bed, the house breathing its emptiness in the dark. What to do on your own in a house you have always shared?

The pavement is still wet from last night's rain but there is someone sitting on it. She has to swerve to get past and slightly recoils. She glances down, irritated and repulsed. A man in dusty jeans, hood pulled up to hide his face; he is eating out of a paper bag. He has a long-haired dog curled beside him on a square piece of printed cardboard, a dog bowl with water in it and an upturned hat in front. Once beggars were a rare sight in Warmfield. Now they are part of the cityscape. Christine would never drop a coin into a begging hat. There is a system to help people, if they want to be helped. In several doorways in the centre, there are sleeping nests of paper and rags. There is a young girl sitting beside the beggar. But she looks ordinary, cleaner, her jacket smarter; she doesn't look like a street person or a druggie. Christine wonders if the girl could be showing support or sympathy, but why? Why would anyone sit on the damp ground on this chilly day? The girl looks young. Christine walks on.

Could it be that Ray was sitting on a pavement somewhere, homeless, hopeless? A ridiculous idea. Her husband would not join the bottom layer, the ones who collected like rubbish or wine lees, the drug addicts and the lost ones. She hesitates as she approaches the corner outside the Ridings where the Romanian woman sells *The Big Issue*. Christine usually swerves around in the other direction to avoid her eyes which search out sympathy and an opening from the passing faces. It is a dilemma, thinking that she has a moral duty, that she should buy a copy while, at the same time, she is repulsed and does not want to get near her. The woman is swaddled in long clothes, her feet covered by her skirts, her head wound with a scarf, everything a different colour. She has pale skin and even features. In *The Big Issue* there are columns with details of 'missing' people. Ray's photo could go in there. This terrible thought brings her to a stop. With an effort she walks on, head down, past the woman seller and through the automatic doors into the shopping centre.

Careful, conscientious Ray is absent. He has gone somewhere, vanished, disappeared. He could not have descended into destitution like those people. Whatever he was doing, wherever he was, he was someone who would always make sure he was safe, comfortable. He had always been careful about himself, himself first but careful for her too.

Now he has left her. Left her alone without safety or comfort. She has not rung the College yet. She knows she must.

Walking, walking, it tricks her mind from its repetitions, its demands and questions. One homeless man and a girl seen fleetingly and she is on the treadmill again.

The GPs surgery is a new building, with a grand, high ceiling in the waiting area, a large play pen full of toys, and the receptionist safely behind glass. She has often reflected that the doctors must be wealthy property owners, with the value of both buildings and land in the bank for them. The design of the interior ensures that waiting patients are too far from each other for much eye contact. People sit in pairs or alone, looking at the floor or reading the electronic notices moving

17

across the walls: a missed appointment costs money, see the nurse for minor complaints. There is no communal experience; each individual is only conscious of themselves. No one looks ill, no one looks hurt or in pain. Pain is unseen. She sits with her hands clasped on her lap. Like her, they have invisible hurt, wounds only they know.

The doctor comes to the door at the edge of the waiting room and calls her name. As she walks across, she knows he is assessing her, judging how she is doing, how badly or well she is coping. The professional observation. Self-consciously she keeps her head high, but does not meet his eye.

'Now, Mrs Callaghan. How can I help today?'

A stock phrase, used even though he knows my situation. He was called, by whom she is unsure, and came to the house to see her in the first days. He offered sleeping pills, which she refused, shook his head sadly and left. A youngish man, handsome, but with nothing behind his professional eyes.

She intended to ask now for sleeping pills to get her through the nights. But a hot sensation inside her rises into her throat.

He arranges his features into a sympathetic gaze.

'This must be very hard for you. I gather there is no news?'
She shakes her head.

'How are you sleeping? Can you manage a few hours?'

She could tell him about the empty darkness and her desperation.

'I could give you a mild antidepressant. It might help.'

He has already turned, tapping on the screen, recording her, preparing the prescription that will signal to her to leave his room.

The hot anger in her chest has reached her face, is burning her head.

'Try this for a couple of weeks. Come back if you still…'

She takes the green and white form out of his hand and leaves the room before he can finish. She hasn't spoken.

By the parked car she stands still. She is overcome by the sense of being a stranger. It is as if a space has opened around her, a fury that separates her from the tarmac, the building, the other patients coming and going through the door. No one can see her standing there. She is invisible.

Later, she thinks perhaps the doctor was overwhelmed by her feelings pulsing in the room. Perhaps he could not cope with such sorrow. No one can cope with it. No one wants to.

At the hospital, she begins to notice details that she might once have been too busy to see. She is transfixed by the movements of a small child in a pushchair, arms and legs flailing as it seeks to break out. She sees the dirt on a man's sleeve as he stretches to pass her an appointment letter. She pauses to watch a colleague using a locker for her personal belongings and she sees the weariness in her arms as she pushes the handbag further in. The ceaseless to and fro of the corridors, the crowded lifts, the cheerful composure of the volunteers directing confused and pained survivors, it has all become intensely colourful and clogged with feeling. She stops on her routes to watch and listen.

One day, she notices a couple sitting in the main waiting area, under the screens which tell people their clinic appointments are due. It is a sterile place with the information displayed as in an airport, efficient and impersonal. A girl is stroking a young man's ear. Her arm reaches sideways to caress one earlobe. He tilts his head slightly to lean into her with a dreamy expression on his face. From behind, Christine watches. The sensual stroking goes on, without embarrassment, although other waiting patients can clearly see them. The girl is giving comfort; he is receiving it. Tender touch in public. Christine feels as if she has intruded on a private intimate act. Would Ray have ever wanted her to stroke him like this? Has she ever used touch, her professional skill, to comfort him, except in the marital bed? This thought makes her flush and she hurries on to the Department.

'How you doing, Chrissie? You ok? You seem a bit quiet these days.' Paveen is looking at her closely, brown eyes enquiring for the truth. Christine knows she is moving more slowly on her rounds, is absent-minded between patients. She can not resist Paveen's kindness for too long.

At last, questioned gently again, she says, 'Ray and me, we are not together anymore. He has left me.'

Paveen nods slowly as if this makes sense of what she has observed, begins to frame another question. But she sees Christine's expression and is quiet. The message will be relayed around the Department. One day, her Head, Liz, stops her and offers her time off 'if she needs it.' Christine thanks her but is unable to tell anyone what it is she needs.

Early one morning, she sits up groggily in bed. The phone has woken her. But it stopped ringing as she reached for it on the bedside table. There is no message. She has been waiting for a message, a phone call, to find out what he is doing, why he is doing it, but there is no word from him. She knows nothing more.

Her chest hurts. Her breathing is short.

'What is happening?' she asks aloud.

There is a surge of pain behind her eyes, in her lungs, in her ears. She pushes back the covers and goes downstairs, wrapping her dressing gown around her. The kitchen light snaps on, making her blink. The windows are dark, the floor cold. She stands in the doorway looking into her empty home. The street is quiet, the gardens neat except for one house where a landlord has put in temporary tenants who let the bins overflow and put broken pieces of household stuff outside: a chair with no back, a box of unknown objects. Some of the neighbours complain. She and Ray always 'made allowances' and held on to their own privacy behind the doors. Now they could all talk about her, the woman whose husband upped and left. Must have had a good reason, seems nice, but you never know, do you? She could be one of those abusers you read about, she could be impossible to live with.

Yes, perhaps I was, she muses, her feet on the chilly tiles, perhaps he couldn't stand it any longer—our comfortable, safe, childless life. No one to please but themselves. How often they had reassured each other with that consolation, especially after a Sunday afternoon with friends whose children ran noisily around and demanded unceasing attention.

He had never accepted her emptiness; he talked cheerily of the good things, the advantages for them as a couple: money, freedom, time. And he kept quiet when she wanted outrage and sorrow.

'He was unhappy,' she says to herself. 'But I thought he was happier than me.'

The sky lightens slowly; each day is shorter and gloomier. It is Saturday, she realises; no work. The pain she knew as rage subsides. What she needs is a plan. Ray had a plan that excluded her. Her next visit to her mother is due. She must make the effort. Her mother is sharp-tongued and sharp-eyed, even in her seventies. She likes Ray most of the time because he is clever; teachers are clever in her book—in a good way and, when it suits her, a not so good way. Christine will have to tell her a convincing story to explain why he has not arrived with her. He often absents himself from these visits but she usually has a reasonable account of some necessity requiring his presence elsewhere.

She sits at the new kitchen table. It is a replacement for the original cheap version, a build-it-yourself he had struggled to put together. She had chosen it in the window of the best furniture shop in town before persuading Ray that they needed a new one. She takes a large sheet of paper and writes a list.

Sell the house. Move to those streets of old terraces nearer the hospital. Change the locks in the mean time. Tell everyone I am divorcing Ray. See a lawyer. Make sure he can't get the money in our savings—move them into new accounts.

Her pen is scratchy and leaking biro ink. Irritated, she stands to find another.

Chapter Three

The waiting area for the morning clinic is full, with its mixture of tense faces and awkward limbs. As she passes through, one couple on the plastic chairs catches her eye. He is tall and handsome with a smooth, shiny head, below which a luxurious beard, extravagant and lush, mocks his scalp: as if his hair has migrated to his chin. Beside him there is an equally striking girl. Christine realises she has almost come to a standstill in amazement. Her eyes travel up from smart tan boots to the long legs, then a quick rush to the blonde head. The girl is wearing shorts. The sheer black tights under the shorts are shaped to look like suspenders, so her thighs are revealed. It is impossible not to look down and dwell. Each swelling length of flesh is tattooed in a different, elaborate picture, all reds and blacks, faces and swirls, symbols and signs, dark and threatening. She has to make herself walk by.

What does it mean, all the ugly paintings? Piercings and displayed flesh? Is flesh no longer private, personal, fresh? In the town, tattoo and piercing parlours are filling the empty shop fronts, vacated by small businesses. 'Dark Power, Voodoo Valour'. The names themselves suggestive of ugliness and pain. She thinks it is as if this is an alien tribe come among them, proliferating, breeding in underground caverns before coming up to daylight.

There is a little huddle of other physios by the doorway as she goes through to the examination area. They are exchanging glances, looking at the girl and her companion. Paveen throws her a look of complicit recoil mixed with amusement. She is relieved someone else is shocked. How shameful to have such thoughts. Either one of them might turn out to be a new patient. There is no judgement to be made about patients. 'We see all sorts here,' is the staffroom mantra. They do. All sorts. Her revulsion is a secret never to be observed. On her day off, she makes herself walk into town, as if leading a normal life. She is used to seeing patients she recognises, sometimes a person she has spent a considerable time with over several appointments. Luckily, they rarely see her, the professional out of uniform with her hair loose. Now there is the risk of meeting one of Ray's colleagues. She knows a few by name, but none well. Maybe they will nod and pass on, without speaking. A dread fills her, each time she sets off, that someone who knows where he is, why he has gone somewhere else, will acknowledge her, will approach with a friendly question, 'how he is doing?' She still has not rung the College to find out basic information. She cannot face the humiliation of admitting he has gone without her knowing. How can she ask the Head of Department, Malcolm, where he is, what he is doing? She thinks of Brenda, who shared classes with Ray. He was fond of her, a woman with a disabled child and a supportive husband. The kind of person whom others talk to, who is reliable and practical. Perhaps she knows, perhaps the whole Department knows that Christine has been deceived, tricked, abandoned without explanation and are already pitying her.

You have to keep looking down as the pavements are so uneven, patched and pitted, scarred where new pipes have been laid or there are patches of repair, cracks and lines and overlapping shades of grey. They are no longer properly maintained by a council short of money. The spots of chewing gum are revolting once you start to notice; they make a random pattern, once juicy with saliva and now integrated darkly into the tarmac.

She walks past the old people's flats, which her mother is still mentioning at every opportunity, and turns onto College Grove Road towards Savile Street. She raises her eyes past the smooth, green grounds of the private school. In the road ahead, a ginger and white cat is lying on its side as if resting. But the angle of its head suggests otherwise. Christine looks quickly away and prepares to cross before she reaches it. Clearly it has been struck by a car and its life is over. A man is using his phone on the pavement nearby. As she approaches, he signals to her.

'Will you help me, please? I can't carry it and my bags as well.' She stops but says nothing.

' Sorry, we don't know each other but can you help?'

'I think it is going to—there's no point,' she protests.

'It's still alive. I'm going to take it to the vet.'

She looks and sees dark blood spread over the tarmac. As she tries to look away, the cat gives a soft cry of pain.

She is conscious of wanting to leave the scene. Cats get knocked down on roads. This one will die soon. This man has no claim on her. Nor does the cat. Suspicion tries to edge her feet away, around the tableau but common politeness tethers her to the spot, momentarily. The man indicates his bags and coat.

'If you could follow, please.'

A boy in blue and grey uniform appears from the school with a flat sheet of cardboard and a large metal tray. He puts them on the pavement before disappearing. Has the man been into the school already to ask for help with his mission? She takes small glances to one side, reluctant to embrace what is happening, while he rolls the cat with extreme gentleness onto the cardboard and then onto the tray. He starts up the side road, with each step his body expressing a lesson in care. She bends, picks up a large zipped bag and a smaller cloth one on top, and follows.

He wears scuffed trainers, worn at the back, scarcely holding at the front; a quilted anorak with the collar turned up to suggest not the bravado of the toffs but something else. The jacket is not thick enough for this cool windy day. She is self-conscious with her burden of strange bags, but he is at ease in his role of rescuer. All the way along the road, over at the crossing, oblivious to the surprise on the faces of passers-by, he talks in a quiet voice, murmuring reassurance to the dying animal. She tries not to meet anyone's eye. She walks stiffly behind him. At the main road, he has to stop for minutes to let the traffic pass, but his soft murmurs never falter. She stands by him, but a few paces away. At last the vet's building is in sight. He speeds up and goes into the reception, without hesitating or looking back at her. Uncertain, she lingers on the pavement, shifting the weight of his bags to relieve her arms. After a few minutes she follows him inside. A pungent tang of dog and wet fur and fear strikes her nostrils. There are two people sitting with their pet boxes, staring incuriously, but there is no sign of the cat rescuer. She sits, putting his bags on the floor and looking away from the other faces.

A dog barks somewhere in the building. Everyone in the room looks up tensely, then relaxes back into stillness and silence.

The door opens and the young man reappears. He comes across to her and shows her a piece of paper. 'I am really sorry,' he says in a rush, 'but they need this to be paid now. I am sorry. Can you lend me the money. Just for now. I promise I will pay it back.'

His eyes meet hers. He is pleading, but at the same time he is confident that she will agree. He thinks it is okay to ask me to pay for his madness. She begins to shake her head firmly, but the other eyes in the smelly room are fixed on her too. Uncertainly she makes a show of reaching into her bag.

'I'm sorry. I'm not sure I have that much in cash.'

She has only glanced at the bill quickly, but how could it be that they charged so much to kill a dying animal?

'They will take a card,' the young man says. His gaze is so direct it is disconcerting; his eyes are a clear blue.

Her retreat blocked, she tries to act as if this is something she can do with grace. The girl at the reception desk has said nothing, has hardly looked at her. Perhaps she thinks I am his mother? Christine wonders acidly.

Once outside he introduces himself as Robin. She passes back the bags.

'These are heavy,' she says as she turns away. 'What have you got in them?'

' I am sorry. It's my shopping and I have been to the library, too. I try to do it all in one trip. Please let me take them. I am sorry. You are so kind.'

He blocks her escape by holding out his hands with an air of serious formality and asks for her name and address so that he can repay her.

'There is no need,' she says. 'No, it is fine. Let's just leave it.' She wants to get away.

'There is a need. Really. You helped me. You have been so good, I am so grateful.'

He is tall, but he keeps his head in a gentle dip towards her. Nervous energy runs through his limbs; he is never quite still, always on the verge of jerking away or starting to run. Even his speech is fast, although hesitant, so she has to wait while he overcomes a pause and then rushes on to the end of a sentence. He is a boy, she thinks. A young man, really a boy. Ray would have no sympathy for this extravagance over the death of a cat, which was going to die anyway. He would have walked past the cat; if asked, he would have refused to help at all.

But she has got this far and the young man's honesty makes it difficult for her to resist his entreaties. It will be a mistake to tell him where she lives, but it seems she must.

'Have you got any paper?' she asks

'Yes, I always have my notebook with me.' He scrabbles in his bag and hands over a small notebook, its cover scratched as if it had been rubbing against hard surfaces.

Slowly, with her reluctance still heavy, she turns the pages to find a blank one and writes her name and address. Ray would be horrified.

'I can't say, can't promise how soon I can get it but I will.' He looks at her so earnestly that she has to look away. It is a large sum. Could this scruffy lad put his hands on it?

Reading her face, he says, 'I will bring it to you even if it takes me, well, a week or so. And it was worth it, wasn't it? At least Horatio had a good end, swift and painless. We did that for him. Together.'

She avoids his eyes, embarrassed by his sincerity and something else she does not understand. Horatio, he has named that poor creature with this elaborate, classical name.

'Death,' he says, just as she is turning away, 'it needs to be…' there is a pause so long she wonders if he has stopped talking and she can go, 'it needs to be quick.'

Chapter Four

Gillian comes at the weekend with homemade biscuits, wholemeal crumbles, full of brown goodness, and insists on putting them out on a plate. She sits with the plate for a 'proper talk.'

Surely nobody else bothers with brown flour for biscuits. Nobody else bothers to make them either. What is she doing here? Christine wonders.

'You must see a solicitor and make arrangements. Get your affairs sorted. You have given him long enough.' This last with a reach across the table to take her hand and a lowering of her voice.

'Long enough? For what?'

'Well—to see,' Gillian hesitates, a ripple of uncertainty across her forehead.

'I don't want to be premature. But really, do you think he is coming back?'

Christine stands in one swift movement, knocking the chair back. She breathes hard as she looks out of the window, her back to the room. She thinks of the list that was never written.

'Oh, I am sorry. Is it too soon? Eddie said it might be, that I should wait. But you know, only a friend can tell you the truth.'

Gillian's confidence has gone. She comes to her and clumsily puts her arms around her back. The hug is warm, a momentary comfort but Christine shrugs away.

'He may be ill, desperate. He might have had a breakdown of some kind. He might just.'

'Of course. We must give him more time to contact you, to let you know.'

The two women stand at an awkward distance. Christine looks out of the window, unseeing. Her friend is another stranger who has no idea what to do.

But she is the stranger. She is the unknown one in the room, her thoughts, her self, hidden and inexplicable.

How could she say the words in her head? That she had no clue what had happened. That she had never known the man she had lived with for two decades. She has no idea what she had been feeling or doing or thinking. So how could she know what he had been feeling, what life he had. How could she say she knew anything about him, what kind of person he was, when she doesn't know anything about herself, what kind of person she is?

Her marriage has been a charade, a parade, vanished in smoke like a trick played by unseen magicians. She is left stranded, unknowing, an audience of one in an empty theatre.

Through the kitchen window she can see leaves collecting on the lawn. A few days earlier, they were on the branches, richly coloured in the sunlight. Now they are sodden, drab, a nuisance on their grass. Ray would collect them at the weekend, a job he likes and loathes. At first he would enjoy being out of the house, useful and active with an end in view. Then he would be tired and bored as the leaves continued to fall, to mock his efforts.

The door bell rings. On the doorstep he stands, jiggling from foot to foot, mumbling rapidly, so quietly she can't understand at first.

'Robin, you came.' It sounds stupid and maybe rude.

Behind her, Gillian has followed, peering, wondering what this young man could possibly be doing here.

'Come in,' Christine says firmly. 'Come in, it's fine, come through to the kitchen for a cup of tea.' Her own boldness is a surprise.

He shakes his head and insists he has only come to hand over the envelope he is holding out. Gillian pushes forward, almost into Christine's shoulder. The three of them are standing together on the doorstep. He smiles at Gillian and holds out his hand. He has good manners, she thinks. But I only invited him into my house to show off to Gillian, who is taking the offer of a hand shake with startled politeness.

'How do you do. I am Gillian, Christine's friend.'

'Pleased to meet you.' he replies in his odd, nervous way, looking directly at her face, 'I am Robin.'

Gillian is flustered.

'Thank you, Robin,' Christine says as calmly as she can. Any minute, she thinks, I shall laugh.

He retreats down the drive and walks away. They both watch him as he disappears along the street towards the corner and the main road. Gillian looks at the envelope but Christine offers no explanation.

'Well, I suppose I had better be off. Are you sure you don't want me to stay a little longer?'

Christine feels a kind of defiance in refusing to explain who Robin is and what is happening.

'Bye then. Take care. Ring me, ring me soon.'

In the envelope is a ten pound note. The first instalment, she supposes.

Within the hour, Gillian rings.

'Chrissie, I had to ring to check you are alright. I thought that man, well he looked, a bit disreputable. Is he a patient? He is very young.'

Christine keeps her voice light. 'No. He is a young friend of mine. You don't need to worry. Thanks for ringing.'

As she cradles the phone, she is surprised to realise that she is smiling.

Last May, she and Ray had spent a week walking in the Dales. She loved the soft green and grey of those fields and hills, the pattern of stones and the brown sugar rivers crashing over the falls with buttery golden foam. 'This is my favourite place,' she said to Ray as they set out from the bed and breakfast one morning, the mist rising. 'Don't you just love it?'

He had introduced her to walking for pleasure. Her mother's idea of a walk is a trip around the supermarket aisles. When she was little, her father would drive them to the east coast so the three of them could walk up and down the concrete promenade, eating pink sugar spun into clouds, or hot waffles with syrup. If the wind was not too strong, they would sit on the sands or stroll a little further along the water's edge. Ray's walking was what she understood educated people do, knowing how to read the symbols on an ordinance survey map, able to plan which footpath to take and how to achieve a circle back to the car. He had given the Dales to her as a gift in their early courtship which thrilled her again and again. It made her feel free to be in this countryside, apparently unchanging, although she knew, as Ray informed her, it was in fact being hollowed out by holiday cottages and farming losses.

She was ahead of him on the grassy path. Cow parsley foamed along the hedges. The path wound between the trees above the placid brown water and came out into fields where tiny glimpses of colour were wild flowers, red campion, meadow buttercups and eyebright, nodding among tall hay grasses. 'Look a meadow, a real meadow.'

Behind her, Ray gave a small grunt of assent. He doesn't appreciate flowers, she thought. I am just talking to myself. Does he feel the wonder of this place at all?

Irritated by his silent plodding, she turned with her arms outstretched and encouraged him towards her. He smiled absently in response and, having the chance to walk past and go ahead of her, went on without stopping, head down, pace as slow as ever.

He did like to walk, she muses. He used to organise our weekends away or weekend hikes. He was not interested any more in other kinds of holidays that I might suggest. That Turkish coach holiday was our last one. I talked him into that. He never said he didn't want to go walking any more, but did he express enthusiasm as I did? He loved arriving at the bed and breakfast; he would laze in bed, for what remained of the afternoon, with a newspaper he had picked up in a village shop. He would exclaim, 'That's really comfortable, great.' There was always tea and coffee, plus homemade biscuits if you were lucky. She would investigate the range of smellies in the bathroom and decide to relax her aching legs in a bath self-consciously revelling in a small experience of luxury, hoping for fun and shared pleasure. But he lay there, reading and not talking.

On Saturdays she always made the effort to go into the city. It is her home and the centre is only a short walk from the house. She went to school here, to the school that used to be in the middle of the park, now an off-shoot of the College. She is part of Warmfield, a 'Warmy girl' and wants to support it, to see it as a place worth living in. One by one, the shops are emptying, becoming shells or worse, new credit or cash 'shops' for the desperate. TO LET signs are massing above the empty windows and the littered pavements. Resolutely, Christine resists depression, chooses not see what is shabby, decaying, the evidence in the streets of people marked now by poverty. She walks briskly past the parents drinking out of cans while the baby squirms its legs and cries, ignores the young huddles laughing on the cathedral wall when they should be in college or school. She still tries to buy their fruit and vegetable supplies in the market, even though there are only two of those stalls now and one sells bowls for a pound a time, with produce that is soft and bound to rot.

The city is scarred and muddled by its past, its cohesion gone. Where once shops and flats huddled along the streets, with a variety of facades from splendidly confident Victorian banks to ancient cottages, a shopping centre projects its steel and glass roof into the air to demonstrate how far into the modern world the city must aspire. The old market hall, shabby but busy, with its green clock tower, went some time ago and the brutal shell that replaced it is already marked for removal too. Its high black roof and block pillars were once thought by the planners to be architecturally significant, but few people linger under their shadow. The rents are so high that many stalls vanished along with the ornate Victorian clock. A ring road pours traffic in new directions and, at the crossing into the bus station, young men, with no other risk or challenge to face, outrun the cars. Their strength is built in a gymnasium and with huge cans of protein supplements, where once it came from sweated labour underground.

Ray might come with her. On a mild sunny day she might cajole him to have a coffee in one of the cafes, although he always thought it was better to go home and have one for free. She would feel glad that they were out in their world enjoying themselves.

As she uses a duster on already clean surfaces, she thinks that he had not come shopping with her for months, even refusing when there was a Craft Fair, or a Food Event in the Bull Ring, some special day organised by the council to attract people into the town centre, even when she more or less pleaded for his company. What had they done together recently? The Saturday evening walk to a pub for an early drink had been one of their regular pleasures. She stands in the living room, her hand on the back of the sofa and cannot remember the last time he had suggested an outing. Friends had invited them out; so they went but otherwise?

'He might as well be dead,' she said aloud.

'I wish he were. I hope he is.'

Chapter Five

In front of their house there is a cherry blossom tree. It has extravagant pink flowers, each as delicate as if it has been made by hand.

Ray disapproved. 'Too frothy,' he had once said.

She saw that he thought it vulgar. She loves it in late Spring when it explodes into bloom. She loves it when the flowers are blown down and lie on the grass in a circle, like a discarded dress. It has grown too near the house, its roots stretching towards the walls and its branches brushing the living room window. It blocks the light when in full leaf. Now, as the next season begins in earnest, its bare branches form a twisting pattern and pale winter sunlight gilds the rug and glances off the surface of the coffee table.

Directly opposite, a new house had been built the year before. The land it stood on had been a garden for the bungalow. When the old lady died her family sold the garden as a building plot and got planning permission to build on top of the bungalow to make it a two storey house. It is now a children's nursery, full of young women and babies by day, dark and still at night. The building work on the new plot started with a survey and some digging. A huge mineshaft was revealed, a breathtakingly deep round hole at the front.

'That's them stumped,' said Ray with satisfaction. 'They can't build on there.'

The shaft was capped and tarmaced over to make the driveway of an enormous new house, built at the back of the plot. With no garden at the back, a huge balcony jutted over the double garage at the front. Two recliners appeared in between large stone lions where an elderly couple might be seen on a warm day.

'The hideous hotel,' Ray called it.

He regretted that they had never challenged the planning application. He was convinced that, if he had taken the time to check the plans, he might have stopped the monstrosity.

But those people had to live somewhere, she thought. The design was grandiose, but it was interesting to imagine what the man and his chain smoking wife thought as they pulled themselves up the exterior staircase and went in through a double front door. Did they feel the shakiness of the ground below? Did they listen for creaks and cracks and wonder in the small hours if the whole house was about to descend into the pit of the earth?

The old man had always waved at her if they passed so she would nod and wave back.

Under these houses, under the city and its suburbs, there is a network of mining tunnels and shafts. The industry has gone, the cacophony of the grinders, the clank of the pit railway, the creak of the lifts taking men underground, gone. But the honeycomb dug out by men over centuries remains. Subsistence is always a word on surveyors' lips. There is a mining museum where visitors can go down in the thundering clamour of the lift to experience the darkness and try to imagine the claustrophobia. My house stands on ground that is not solid, she thinks today.

She goes swiftly in and out of the door and focuses on her direction. She is careful not to meet eyes. Her neighbour has made attempts to catch her as she leaves or arrives. This is a woman with a face for smiling, ready to be friendly. Christine parks the car, walks with her head down and almost runs to the door, refusing to see curiosity and kindness stretched towards her. She has entered a tunnel, a dark place where no one can join her.

She does wait for Robin. For two weeks there is no sign. Perhaps he will let the debt drift or drop altogether. Perhaps he cannot manage the money. She has no real idea of his circumstances.

Finally, he is on the doorstep with his envelope in hand. He is like a pony, she thinks, he needs coaxing.

'I have just made tea. Please come in and have a cup. It's so cold today.'

'You are kind. Very kind.'

In his hesitating way he lets her lead him into the kitchen. He stands looking around with interest. What is she doing inviting him in? What on earth would Ray say if he saw that she has brought a strange person, a man, into the house? He is clean at least. He does not smell.

'You have a very nice house, Christine.' He uses her name as naturally as if they are well-known to each other. A little shock goes through her. How does he know what she is called?

Seeing the confusion she cannot conceal, he says, 'Oh sorry. Was that rude? I really didn't mean to, sorry, it is only because…'

'Because I wrote my name down for you. Of course. It's fine, Robin.'

'Please sit. I will pour the tea.'

He sits at the table where she has indicated, running a hand absently through his sandy hair.

'I didn't mean to take up your time. I just want to explain. I can only give you the money in instalments, you see.'

'That's fine, Robin.' She sits opposite and looks calmly into his face. 'What were you planning, exactly?'

'Planning, that's the hard part. The Job Centre, I have to go every day now. They won't let me do my voluntary work, so it's all a bit tight.'

He spreads his hands in weary acceptance. Long fingers, she notes.

'What voluntary work were you doing?'

'At the Arts Centre, you know the one in the old library. I like writing, I thought I could write some materials for them, to explain and describe what happens in each of the workshops. Anyway, it was useful to them for me to cover reception sometimes, or help out moving boxes. I go every day. Well. I went. Now I have to show I am applying for jobs every day, at the Job Centre.'

'Can't you tell them you are getting useful experience at the Centre? Challenge them?' It does not seem to Christine that he had been doing anything very useful, but clearly it matters a great deal to him.

'You have to be careful. Not upset anyone. If they think you are being difficult, it means sanctions—and that means no money.'

35

Christine is torn between feeling this young man's situation is unfair and alarm. Why has she got a jobless man sitting in her kitchen, one of the workless, perhaps workshy, dependent on the state, taking benefits although in his twenties?

'I am so grateful you helped me that day. Really, you're so kind.'

The emphasis on her kindness prickles under Christine's skin. She thinks herself a critical, suspicious person who only let him into her house the first time because she wanted to spite an old friend, someone who is kind.

He leans across the table and reaches out a hand to take hers. Her slight withdrawal stops him from grasping it.

'I can't pay you back the money in one go. If you agree, I can let you have it regularly, as often as I can manage it. I promise I will pay it all back.'

She nods agreement.

'How long have you lived here, Christine?'

'Five years, no, six now. We lived in Losset before.'

'Do you like it better here?'

Her hands are tense as she holds out the mug to him. This is not a conversation she should be having with him. Is he trying to find out about her? Could he be 'casing the joint'? The quaint expression rings in her inner ear. Everyone warns that is what strangers, intruders, may do. He has sandy-coloured hair which sticks up from a high forehead as if he is always pushing it back.

'What about you, Robin?' Determinedly she sits across from him, clasping the mug of tea she doesn't want to drink.

'I live in my mother's house in Holbury. I have lived there, well, me and my mother and my brother have lived there since I was nine. I left to work in York but I came back when Mum was ill.'

'That's nice. Is your brother at home at the moment?' She sounds false, has no idea why she is asking him this question. He has not explained his plan to pay the money back but Christine assumes he has brought another instalment. She must take the envelope he has already put onto the table and get him to leave.

'My brother lives abroad. Hong Kong at the moment.'

His eyes meet hers with no guile, encouraging Christine to ask more questions. They sit in silence for a few minutes.

'How has your week been?' she asks.

'Not too bad, not too bad. Just form-filling mostly.'

'Form-filling?' she queries.

'Every day you have to sit there and fill in a form.' He gives her his nervous smile.

'At the Job Centre? Isn't there anything for you? Nothing suitable?'

'Not really. They push me to go to interviews, you know: to fill in the form you have to show you have done an interview. Warehouse jobs. Petrol forecourt. But I have done that, so they don't push it much.'

'You have done petrol forecourt jobs? What happened?'

'They harassed me. Just pressure to do longer and longer shifts. There are never enough staff so they try and make you work more and more hours. They need to employ more people, but they won't. Always doing it on the cheap. All these jobs are like that.'

'What did happen then?'

'I walked. Couldn't stand the bullying. Of course, then you don't get any benefit for weeks because you chose to leave.'

'Oh dear.' She knew this was an inadequate response but she could not think of what to say.

He smiled and ate the rest of his biscuit.

'Have you got any certificates, Robin? Any qualifications at all?'

'A maths degree.'

She swallows the shock of surprise she feels.

'Surely that could lead to something better than those kinds of jobs. Something better for you.'

He shrugs as if this is a philosophical problem he is unable to solve. He stands. 'I must go. Thank you, Christine. You are really kind.'

As he reaches the front door, he turns and smiles his jangly smile with all his limbs somehow in concert with his intention.

'See you next time. I will keep the instalments going. Thank you again for the tea.'

On the television and the radio there are incessant reports of new violence, 'outbreaks of hostilities' in the commentators' jargon, in cities and regions of unending war, Syria, Lebanon, Afghanistan. We are forced to watch their horrors, people bombed out of their homes, children's faces blank with fear, refugees on the roads and the seas. She turns off the voices coming into the house, refuses to see the images.

Why do we have to know? she asks the screens. Is there not enough cruelty here? Her eyes sting. Out there, hideous acts of deliberate human cruelty. Here, in my comfortable, lovely home, who sees the cruelty left here?

How could he peel away our life and take my skin with it? Leave me on my own with the windows full of eyes looking in? Every day has the same pattern. The routine of work makes it possible to get up and go out, to take action. She believes in her skills, in the power of her hands and learning, the degree she chose to risk after years of tedious, low-level work. She had thought of herself as an average person, not as clever as those who achieved at school but there she was, studying biology and science, learning a profession and craft she puts into practice with pride. She enjoys what her hands and her knowledge can do, how they smooth a muscle, reshape a limb, teach the body to relearn and heal—the child who has to painfully stretch her leg every day if she wishes to walk with her foot to the floor, the man with the broken wrist who will make a full recovery if he learns how to straighten the hand at right angles, the slow recovery of an accident victim or someone disabled by a stroke. She can give the gentle push, the persistent encouragement, the professional smile of assessment. She avoids mess, agony, involvement even though these are so present. She leaves them to the nurses and assistants chatting over the bedpans. She likes her job for the clean smooth finish, the completed record, the job done as far as, and only as far as, it can be.

Her refusal to discuss anything about herself, a new layer of defence on top of her habitual restraint and discretion, has driven even Paveen into acceptance. There are caring stares, as she labels them, and occasional whispered gossip, smothered as she approaches, but she is left alone. So Christine can be this self, the professional who works calmly and pleasantly with her patients, doing her duty and using her expertise.

Sometimes, the rage swells in the middle of a consultation but she has learnt to swallow it. If she is lucky there will be a lunch or coffee break giving her time to stand outside, to stand on the bitterest day and throw silent swear words into the air, his name reviled on the wind.

One Sunday afternoon, unable to rest or entertain herself, with time dragging through the day, she begins emptying kitchen cupboards. She gets a large tray and fills it with herb pots, jars of spice pastes, half-opened packets of couscous and tins of tahini. As she clears, she reads labels. She gets a large black bag and starts selecting items to throw away. Working quickly, without contemplation, she throws bottles and jars, packets and tins into the bag, paying no attention to the clink and crash as they fall. Once one cupboard is empty, she puts on rubber gloves and energetically cleans the shelves, rubbing hard at spill rings and marks. Now she puts the things she has saved back. Instead of packed shelves with cooking aids and ingredients lined up and squashed in, she has clean spaces, with a few items. Choice items, she thinks, my choice. No more couscous or hot paprika. The bag of discards clunks noisily as she lifts it. There is lots of glass to be recycled, but resolutely she thinks to herself, I will not wash them out, they shall all go into the dustbin.

Ray liked to cook. She has been proud to mention to friends and colleagues that he did. Paveen was happy to be impressed. But, inevitably, his cooking would be more important than hers; take more time, mean more to him or anyone else, including her. He might go weeks without either suggesting what to eat or showing interest in her careful weekly meal plans. Then a chance viewing on TV or a conversation at work, or most often the weekend papers, set him off on a culinary quest for an ingredient. He would hunt it, pacing aisles in pursuit of the one essential thing. He called it 'sourcing'. If their local supermarket was behind the times and the hunt unsuccessful, off he went to another town, bigger and smarter than Warmfield, where he was sure it could be found. The cooking would involve setting out small bowls, each with a separate part of the 'prep', chopped onions in one, grated ginger in another. Everything carefully measured, weighed, calculated and the magic ingredient in pride of place. 'Who ever heard of sumac,' she queried, but only to herself, 'before this cooking craziness everywhere?' Ray ignored her forays into the kitchen to discover how far he had progressed, pink-faced and steaming over the pots. Once the dish was underway, he would appear in the doorway, brandishing a utensil, and declare an expected arrival time. She would smile and nod, even though so often the waiting period had lengthened past her appetite. When the marinated, aubergines, sprinkled with sumac and roasted to a shiny perfection arrived on a white serving dish, she ate uncomplainingly. Ray talked her through each mouthful, encouraging her to report on the texture, the subtleties of flavour she could detect, the visual effect of the purple on white. He took mental notes, commenting perhaps on the suitability of the dish to give to friends or to record alterations to the original recipe.

Today she takes a small white bowl off the shelf. She breaks two eggs into it and slowly whisks them with a fork. She adds a pinch of salt and a grind of pepper. When the butter bubbles in the pan she pours in the eggs. While the omelette starts to set, she cuts herself a slice of white bread. It is a meal that would disappoint Ray. She enjoys its simplicity. It is clean food. No more heavy mixes of strange spices, no more chickpeas or couscous; from now on, she decides, she is only going to eat what she likes.

Chapter Six

Out of the coach window, she watched the famous honey-coloured landscape of Cappodocia. Earlier, they had scrambled in Monks Valley among these strange protuberances, the wind harsh in their faces; it was a relief to be back on the bus even though it meant more travel, more sitting. This cultural tour of Turkey had involved a lot of sitting. Ray had protested when she found the advert in the Sunday papers, with alluring photos of the 'enchanting fairy landscape' and references to the ancient Roman and Christian sites.

'Only old people go on coach holidays,' he said when she read out the description.

She had persisted. Surely someone who taught history and geography and hated beach holidays must be interested in this package. If she knew there was desperation in her planning, she ignored it. Maybe he did too, she wonders. By then they had not taken a holiday of more than two or three days for three years.

Once they had met the rest of the group at the Turkish airport, three of them young women, one old lady with her daughters in attendance, several middle aged couples a little older than themselves, Ray had enclosed himself in privacy. His shoulders said 'don't talk to me.' It was left to Christine to attempt the right pitch of friendliness. The huge buffet dinners in hotels were a trial. There was so much food that the eye could not take it in. The first time you saw the lavish display it was marvellous to explore: bowls of every kind of condiment and pickle; metal dishes of hot stews and fried things. By the third evening it was clear that the selection was limited. Many of the dishes were raw salads, which they had been advised not to eat, and some of the others were unpleasantly greasy mixtures. The dining rooms were like a huge school canteen, full of tourists in groups and with the same jeopardy of seating. Every evening Christine faced the difficulty of Ray's refusal to sit with anyone else; there were few tables for four and none for two. He simply made his selection and set off for the farthest corner without looking right or left. She found it impossible to avoid the eyes of people she had been chatting to during the day, and hard not to respond to a call of 'do join us.' For two evenings she left him to himself and sat on a big table monopolised by a large woman from the group who taught in a private school in Oxford—'one couldn't trust oneself to a state place'—but she could not make sense of the woman's barrage of information about ancient history. On subsequent nights, she tried with more determination to avoid forced sociability.

She remembers the days of sitting in the coach, watching the landscape pass. Most clearly she remembers the whirling dervishes.

As they neared the last stop of the Dervishes day, she could hear the two couples she had labelled 'posh' talking in front. The women were bony and wore the clothing favoured by those who live in the country, green jackets and silky scarves. The men were as predictable in tweed. The four were comparing the itinerary on the published leaflet with the day's outing.

'Erdun,' the loudest of the women called to the guide, 'we are not getting the trip to the hidden village we were promised.'

'The itinerary,' the young guide, called Erdogan, explained with professional patience for the third or fourth time on this trip, 'is just an outline. If you read the notes, it says we have to make adjustments for the weather and time. Thank you.'

The woman sank back , still muttering to her companions

'Can I talk to you all about the balloon flight.'

A lengthy discussion about the offer of a balloon trip followed, with everyone on the coach participating. Ray showed the first interest she had seen since they started.

Spectacular, the best view of the landscape, the best sights of any balloon flight in the world, see the dawn and have the experience of a lifetime—she had read the pamphlet.

'It's expensive. Are you sure you won't do it?' Ray asked.

'No. I can't do heights like that. You know I can't. Besides it is too much money for two of us. You do it.'

For a while she thought he was going to put his name down. But the moment passed and he shook his head at Erduwan's request. She was disappointed for him. He could have had an adventure, but refused it. She went back to gazing out at the darkening hills.

The coach drew up at the Whirling Dervishes centre, a cement block building, high above the town, with its own car park and a heavy wooden entrance door. The group shuffled into a dark cave-like room where they sat on four sides around a small stage. A man in black robes explained what was going to happen and asked them to be silent. Photographs were forbidden until the end. It was explained that the dancers were ordinary men with jobs, but men who dedicated themselves to this specialised Islamic practice. Everything in nature revolves like the electron and protons in the atoms of all things, they were told, and so the dervishes revolve in unity with all beings. The ceremony represented a spiritual ascent towards perfection.

Christine felt sleepy. It was going to be hard to keep her eyes open. This was a cultural highlight and she must try to pay attention.

Five young men entered the stage in tall head dresses and black robes, which they discarded slowly to reveal stiff white costumes, like paper frocks, and on their heads, tall flowerpot hats. They began their unfolding dance, slowly round and round on delicate feet, turning in a ritual form of meditation. A flute player set the pace in a thin call and a drum sounded a flat note at intervals. Their bodies swung and twirled faster and faster to the music; she could not see their feet. Their arms were folded on their chests when they started, but slowly they held them out in graceful curves, one hand pointing to the earth, one up to God. They created human sculptures, white shapes in motion. Despite her weariness it became impossible not to watch. Their faces were masks of contemplation, eyes unseeing, turned inwards. Then they slowed again, round and round until they were still. Cameras began flashing once the signal for photographs had been given, videos whirred, the spiritual energy dissolved into the dusky air.

The cold mountain wind was a shock after the enclosed room. It was evening, time to go back. Sitting again on the coach, she thought how mysterious the world is, how strange and unknowable that people should choose to spend their time rotating for their religion. As they started the journey back to the hotel and another buffet dinner, she asked Ray what he thought about what they had seen.

'They achieve ecstasy,' he said.

She stared at him, unsettled. She had expected sarcastic dismissal.

That night she moved to make love to him. A bridge between them could surely be spun out of caress and stimulus. He responded to her invitation with speed and vigour. When it was finished, she lay wondering if it was her fault; was she cold hearted, unmoved as she was by the religious dancers and their moving meditation, only able to give her body as a gesture, willed and mechanical? Had she felt ecstasy tonight or ever in their life together? Was religious experience the same as sexual excitement? Why had Ray, who had no religious belief, was not a spiritual person as far as she had ever known, used that word?

She could remember the heat of their first togetherness, even in the early years of marriage, on occasion. But the ending of hope for a child had emptied lovemaking of meaning for her.

She thought of the night, many years ago, when hope had left her.

He had gently put his arms around her in bed and pulled her close.

'I have to tell you something: I know I am fertile.'

The words rang as clear to her now as then. She had squirmed away but he held her more firmly.

'This is hard. I know you will find what I am going to tell you very hard. When I was nineteen, I got a girl pregnant. I've told you about her. Lillian.'

'Lillian,' she cried out.

'The girl I met on holiday.'

'Your first love,' she said into his shoulder.

'Yes, she was. But we didn't plan on a child. Or anything really. She had an abortion. Then we broke up.'

Christine cried softly. Tears fell ceaselessly onto his skin. She pulled away and lay with her back to him. So it was her fault, the months of hoping and hope ending, the clinging to a possibility that never came. They had been talking of a clinic, but kept putting it off. Hadn't her own mother waited ages to start with her; hadn't she said, 'You just need patience.'

At nineteen, Christine had a boyfriend. They were careful, but also careless more than once. How terrified she had been each time, how thankful when the monthly cycle came again, how lucky she thought herself.

Ray did have the ability to make life. He could have a family without her. She is barren, without issue, with nothing to give him but herself. And nothing to give herself.

'I don't want children,' he had said that night, the only time they talked about the great hole in her life, in their lives. 'Listen to me, I didn't want a child then. And I don't now. My life, our life, is enough for me.'

Awake in the middle of an early winter night, the house empty and Ray gone, she listens to the rain on the windows, an unceasing fall of sound. This is the month to prepare for next year in the garden, to plant bulbs for the spring and linger over seed packets, each containing a promise of growth and beauty. She has not emptied her pots or planned what bulbs to buy. She cannot see the next year ahead or imagine the coming of spring.

Later, she sleeps as if at the bottom of deep water, above her a peaceful darkness she accepts. She wakes, forced up into the morning as one word surfaces in her mind. Sabbatical— the word means for a year. He intends to return. The realisation stabs her. He has gone for a year. He intends to come back.

Chapter Seven

She sees that there is a pattern to Robin's visits. He nearly always comes on every second Saturday afternoon in the month. It must be his money situation, when his benefit comes and how he manages it. Perhaps a routine is important to him, too. She sees the blue of his eyes focus intently when she opens the door. He is pleased to see her. He could just post his envelope through the door if she was not there. She begins to plan her own routine to ensure he does catch her in.

By the third Saturday she knows he will come at four in the afternoon. So she organises her time so that she will be there. If Gillian rings to invite her out, or suggest she was free to call in, or if a colleague mentions something that is happening and loosely invites her to come along, she replies, as if regretful, 'Oh dear, I am busy.'

She has refused so many invitations since September that she is gaining the reputation of a recluse. Anyway, what right have they to cajole and query, she wonders. Even Paveen has begun to expect refusal. She cannot control the cooling of their friendship. Gillian is beginning to retreat, ringing less often, accepting her excuses more readily, leaving her opinions behind when she does come.

One Saturday she is ready for him. As soon as she has opened the door, she steps back so that he has to follow her inside. On the kitchen table she has laid blue and white striped mugs, a matching teapot and a plate of biscuits.

'Please sit and have a biscuit.'

He is uncertain of what to do next. After a tiny pause he takes a biscuit and nibbles. They sit in silence for several minutes. She eats a biscuit to keep him company.

'So you live in your mother's house, Robin.' She is conscious of using his name. At work, she avoids too much personal contact with patients. It is not professional to call them by their first names or ask too many questions. Besides the job appeals to her because it is focussed. She helps people tackle specific difficulties. The rest, their illnesses, habits, their problems, are not relevant. She thinks of those areas outside her role as messiness. She avoids mess.

'She left it to me and my brother in her will. He works abroad, so I am there.' He looks into the obvious sympathy on her face.

'Yes, she died, six years ago. Time goes, doesn't it. Once I thought I could never forget her face and—anyway, the house is mine unless Dudley, that's my brother, ever wants to come back.'

'I'm sorry. What happened? She must have been quite young, I mean too young.'

'Too young. She was ill for five years. Really ill, and then they took her into the hospice and told me she would die.' He speaks calmly, but his voice has become lower. He has a long nose and a mouth which suggests gentleness. He bites his lips as he speaks and furrows his forehead.

'I looked after her for five years, but they didn't listen to me. They didn't understand that I knew her and what she needed.'

'How sad for you. Did your brother manage to come home before?'

'He just got there. She waited for him. I knew she would. She had to say goodbye to both of us.'

'I work in a hospital, Robin. I am a physiotherapist.'

'That must be a really interesting job.' He looks at her keenly. 'Do you work up here, at the new hospital?'

'Well, it is the old one in posh new buildings. Same problems but with lots of glass.'

Christine makes another pot of tea and puts more biscuits out on the plate. She is glad she bought the oat ones as he takes another without being asked.

'Excuse me for asking, Christine, but are you married?'

She turns her head to look out at the damp garden through the kitchen window.

'My husband has left me. I don't know where he is.'

This is the first time she uses these words and the first time she has told anyone so clearly. She has not contacted the College, not tried to get in touch again with any of his friends who might know more than she does. It would be humiliating to admit that he has a plan of which she is ignorant. He is the deserter. She is the abandoned.

She thinks Robin is about to express regret for her and perhaps ask her questions. To stall him, she asks again about his mother.

In the quiet of the kitchen, with the background click of the boiler as the flare of the pilot light adjusts, he begins to tell her the story of his mother. She had worked for a long time as a cook in an old people's home.

'She was famous for her cooking,' he says with emphatic pride. 'They asked her to do buffets for the staff, special menus for the Mayoral visit and other celebrations. She sent money to me and my brother at university. She worked and worked. She was so good at her job and they were so mean that they never found a good person to cover her, so she was always working, weekends, all summer. She never had a holiday. All her friends came round with gifts from their trips to sunny places, showed her photos.'

'She never complained, my mother,' he says, his voice rising. 'She didn't complain about anything. She just got on with it. After we left Dad, she had to work to keep us so she just worked all the days she could. Me and Dudley, we didn't realise, not till she went into hospital, not till her friends started telling us. You don't see things as a kid.'

He talks on. Christine listens. His long limbs are still, one hand clasped around the mug, the other loosely curled. His voice is low but steady, as if this is a story he has told to himself many times. His blue eyes are dimmed as he remembers.

'You see, when she went into hospital she just rang us and said she wasn't well. She didn't tell us she had been ill for a long time. She said she was going to have an op and it would be alright. When the doctor told us it was a shock.'

'It was cancer and when they opened her up, it was everywhere. The doctor said it out straight, round the bed with the curtains drawn. It was too late, he said. Dudley nearly dropped. I had to put my arm out. She asked the doctor if she would see Christmas, it was about this time of year, he said he wasn't sure.'

'She lived five years after that. I had five years with her. I had a job in York, I worked with a youth service project—but I went to live with her. Dudley stayed for a while and then he went to work abroad. He had always planned to, teaching you know, and he couldn't cope. Some people can't take sickness. You will know that, Christine, in your job. He came to see her once a year, but he couldn't stand to be in the house for more than a day or two. He visited friends, came back, went off again and then his leave would be over. That was that.'

'She didn't fuss. She knew how he was.'

'So you looked after her for all that time?'

'Yes. You see, they sent her home saying there was nothing to be done. She was going to die. Then a doctor rang. They had had a case conference at another hospital, you know the special cancer place? He offered her an op. Said it would give her years of life. So she agreed.'

'But she suffered so much. They cut so much away. She had horrible symptoms. Pain. She could hardly eat anything.'

'It was wonderful that you could look after her.'

'I did everything for her. I bathed her, I cleaned her up. Christine, I was her eldest son and I had to do all the things no son should do for his mother. But she trusted me. She needed me. So I did it all. She said the doctor boasted that he had given her a life.'

'Christine, sometimes she said to her friends 'This is not a life.' I didn't know that. Not until she was in the hospice. She always talked to me as if she could bear it. As if we could bear it together. But she was living for me and him, not for herself. She kept going for us. Only for us.'

'She spent five years dying so we would have her with us.'

His face has turned in on itself. He has removed himself to another place. Christine sits and lets him sit.

'I didn't want her to go. Even then, when they had told me, when they kept me out of the room, wouldn't listen to me, I tried to keep her here. But it was wrong of me. She needed to go, a long time before that.'

His eyes are startlingly bright as they meet Christine's across the table.

'You were not to know. She protected you. She wanted to be alright for you.' Her words are feeble, but he nods, accepting her need to give reassurance.

'Is your mother alive, Christine?'

'Oh very much so,' she laughs, trying to change the atmosphere in the room, smiling encouragingly at him. 'My mother is a tyrant. She wouldn't make things easy for me. Oh no.'

'Like my Dad then,' he says. 'I must go. Taken up your time. Thank you.'

After he has left, she sits at the table, her hands flat on the surface feeling the smoothness of the wood. Stillness rises from the floor and locks her legs, then her body, so she sits motionless while the boiler clicks. Her eyes look out of the window into the road but she sees nothing. Immobile as a statue, she sits unhearing and unseeing. At last she shakes herself. She looks at her hands, strong and broad for a person with a compact, short body like hers. Thoughtfully, she stretches them out, splays her fingers, admires their whiteness, the neat nails, the sense of capability they express. She gets up, starts to clean the kitchen, to prepare her meal, to fill the space she lives in.

Chapter Eight

As she parks the car, her stomach tightens. All the houses on the estate are sparkling in the dark afternoon. The house next door has a huge Santa in the front garden, a plastic Santa Claus swaying in the chill air and flashing its lights with determined gaiety. Strings of lights like icicles hang from the eaves of the house opposite. Every window has a cone shape of coloured lights framed as a signal to the onlookers. Only her mother's house is gloomy.

'Why no tree, Mum?' she asks as she takes off her coat and puts it on the banister. The coat stand that stood there, when she was a child, has gone, so broken by the weight of old abandoned coats that it met its end on a bonfire.

'Who needs a tree at my age? I've put my cards up.'

There are a pitiful few on the shelf above the gas fire, pictures of robins and the three kings. When her father was alive, Christmas had all the extravagance he could gather in his arms and bring into the house. Her mother has shrunk into a careful resistance, oblivious to any sign she ever had to suffer such a person. The house is full of stale air and emptiness. Falsely cheerful, Christine sits in the green chair, her father's favourite, moves the cushion with feathers coming out of it and smiles. Julie is a small woman, thin with sparse grey hair tied back from her face. She is seventy-seven and looks a decade older.

'How is that husband of yours? I haven't seen him in a while.'

'Ray? He's fine. He's just busy.'

'Too busy to come, I know. Don't worry, he can't be asked to bother with an old woman like me. I understand.

'Mind you, if I lived nearer I might have a chance to see him.'

This is a constant refrain in Julie's campaign to move to one of the old people's houses in Elizabeth Gardens, around the corner. The council house is too big for her and the changes the government is making to the welfare system means she is finding it hard to live there on reduced money.

Moreover, she feels under pressure to leave it so a family can have it. Most of the estate has become private property but Christine's parents were too nervous to make that jump into another class. Her father talked as if he could do it, was going to see it happen, but he never did; it never happened.

On light evenings, this estate was a place of adventure and noise: the calls of children in the wide streets until late; the scraping of knees on the wall into the piece of wasteland, theirs to claim; the boy with the wooden sword who terrorised the younger ones into shrieks and wild dashes; the boy with the go-cart who charged sweets, and later money, for a swoop down Little End, where you would try not to crash into the end of the cul-de-sac. Later, groups of them stood or sat on corners, swapping cigarettes and lipsticks. Coming home was a full stop to the evening that meant listening again to her mother's list of admonishments before escaping upstairs. Her father had been a genial silence in those years, taking his evening meal on a tray in front of the television.

Christine makes tea for them both. As she pulls the knitted cosy over the pot, she calls from the kitchen.

'Actually Mum, Ray is not alright. At least, I don't know how he is. I don't know where he is.'

Julie fusses with the small table by her chair. She moves the pile of *Woman's Weekly* magazines to one side and indicates where the tray can sit.

'The thing is, he has left. Left me, and I have no idea where he is.'

Julie gives no sign she has heard. She pours tea into thin china cups and the saucers rattle in the quiet room.

Christine cannot take the words back. She cannot un-speak them. Her legs feel unreliable. She realises that Julie has closed her eyes. Is her mother going to ignore her? It may only be a second but it seems minutes go by before she opens her eyes and looks directly at her daughter.

'You poor thing. No children and now this. I am sorry for you.'

There is a ripple of warmth across the room, which catches in Christine's chest and moistens her eyes. 'Mum, it's ok. I'm coping.'

'Well, you have no choice. We never have a choice. Just get on and cope, that's the way.'

Christine notes the inclusive 'we'. Does her mother mean women in general or, for once, is she claiming a similarity, a bond, between her and her daughter?

'What about money? Are you alright?'

'I earn my own money. The bills are being paid. He hasn't touched the joint account and so far his contribution has carried on.'

'So he is not dead, then.'

Christine drinks her tea.

'That big house you got yourselves—the mortgage must be a struggle.'

Ray resisted all talk of Julie moving into the old people's places so near to their own home. 'Just too close, for us and for her. She'd get fed up anyway, without those nice neighbours and you and me being out all day.' Christine wonders if her new reality means she must face up to Julie's demand. She is her only family nearby.

'Have you told your sister? What does she say about it?'

Julie has not mentioned Ray's name and says nothing about him. She is interested in the money and in what Susy will say.

She does not ask about my feelings or when it happened and why. I could not tell why. I don't know why. Christine folded her hands in her lap. Her father is the one who would have given her a hug.

Susy is the sayer of opinion, the spoken word of truth for her mother. She has not rung her sister. She has not thought of it. Her younger sister has become the icon; at barely seventeen, she vanished into America on the arms of an older man. She visits every few years, bearing gifts; she sends photos of her four children, now adults. She rings her mother once a month to update her on the family news, which is always good news. Christine has often remembered the old phrase, all her geese are swans.

Years ago, Susy treated their parents to a trip 'out there'. Her father's face showed patient bewilderment at the airport, a place so familiar to so many, but still strange to these two. He was a postman, fascinated by the idea of faraway places whose

53

stamps and postmarks he might see. But the reality of air travel diminished him. He and her mother talked about New York State for a long time afterwards, talking of the marvels of the USA, but they never went again.

Today she has made the first public announcement of her situation. It will be relayed over the Atlantic. She imagines her mother with a megaphone, booming the dreadful news from coast to coast so that everyone can hear, everyone can shake their heads in surprised disapproval. Her sister's reaction will be sugary, American concern, sharpened with tiny shards of blame.

'Before I go, Mum, let's arrange Christmas. I am thinking of doing something different. I might volunteer at the shelter. You know, the one at St Catherine's? Would you mind awfully?'

The words are a surprise. This was an idea she has wondered about only fleetingly. Robin telling her on his last visit that he would spend Christmas Day at the hospice has made her wonder if she can carry on as tradition dictates, if she could do something new. Last year, Ray and her mother played cards in the darkening afternoon while she drank glass after glass. She is not good at cards.

Her mother puts her teacup down with a snap of china.

'Oh, I am sorry. Of course I won't leave you on your own.'

'Christine, you know perfectly well that my lovely neighbours invite me every year and every year I have to say that I must refuse because I owe it to you and Ray to come to your house.'

'I will come and get you on Boxing Day, then, for the panto. Just the two of us. It will be fun.'

'Yes, dear. Fun.'

The neighbours are a couple about Julie's own age, who have adopted her. They have spent considerable sums improving their house, since they bought it, for a song, years ago under the national scheme to encourage private ownership, by giving discounts to existing tenants. They invite Julie to admire it, for tea and occasional Sunday dinners. They call and chat and offer help just as if she were much older and frailer than themselves. Perhaps they have to have a project,

Christine thinks bitterly, now the house is done. Perhaps they are critical of a daughter who only comes once a week and refuses to discuss her mother moving much closer. Soon they will know more about me, so they will be able to list even more shortcomings.

Driving home, Christine laughs. She giggles at first and then laughs out loud, her hands beating in rhythm on the steering wheel. She has extricated herself from another dreary Christmas Day, when she would be the only one making an effort to acknowledge the special occasion. She has been cruel to her mother—oh yes, it is cruel to refuse to see your only parent, to make out you have more important things. She has committed herself to doing something she has never considered, which she always thought is a do-gooding, sad person's response to Christmas, helping at a shelter, dishing out school dinner plates to the homeless and helpless. She thinks she does enough at work to help other people, the halt and the lame especially. She has no need to prove her goodness anywhere else. But the laughter builds inside her like a fountain bursting upwards into the air.

Chapter Nine

In a doorway a young girl is sitting with her scraggly dog on a sheet of cardboard. If she is homeless, how can she afford to feed a dog? Christine asks herself as she feels an anxiety for the girl, a new feeling. The girl has a pale face, long hair scraped back so her scalp shows and tied with string; she could be fifteen or twenty five. Too young, in any case, to be unprotected. Her clothes are shapeless and khaki, not thick enough for a cold pavement in a chilly month. While trying to look as if it is coincidental, nothing to do with the girl herself, Christine fumbles for change in her purse. Quickly, without looking into the girl's face, she tosses coins onto the cardboard.

'God bless,' the girl calls out loudly to Christine's back. 'Thank you, kind lady.'

It is early in the dead section of the year. She has refused invitations to New Year's Eve parties, even the one at Gillian and Eddie's. She grimaced to herself as New Year's resolutions are laughed over by colleagues, no more wine in the week, going to the gym regularly, less time on YouTube and Ebay, losing a few pounds—all the starting points for change which people espouse, while simultaneously recognising the imminence of failure. Christine has no energy for self-renewal, for positive thinking. She is trapped in the present, dreary January stretching ahead into the year, with no card, no letter, no presents, no word from Ray. She signed the usual list of Christmas cards, a task that had always fallen to her, with her own name, only hers. The first one she wrote looked so strange, she hesitated to put it into an envelope. With a sense of conscious significance, she delivered a card to the house next door, and to the horrible hotel over the road, knowing she was giving a message they have been waiting for.

There were fewer cards this year, all the College ones missing; some of the cards that arrived were addressed to them both as usual. Gillian sent her one with a serious and sickly message about strength in adversity. Christine was tempted to tear it up, but instead gave it a prominent place on the mantelpiece. She did not take the artificial tree out of its box.

Her weekends now are pools of emptiness. It is an effort to divide the days so there is some purpose: shop for food, clean the kitchen, read the novel, scan the newspaper. Often she finds herself sitting, doing nothing. The house is still. The boiler makes its noise or a car engine starts in the street outside. Otherwise there is silence.

To rouse herself, she takes walks: a brisk turn around the hospital campus, keeping clear of the buildings; or into the city, into the warm scrum of sales-shoppers rummaging through rails of clothes or standing in front of huge televisions as if transfixed. She buys nothing, speaks to no-one. Sometimes, one of her patients sees her but is uncertain if it could be her, their physio without a white uniform, in this different setting. She meets no eyes, avoids looks, walks on.

Worries about Robin go round and round in her mind. She is conscious that she has no right or necessity to be concerned about him. The money he still owes her is insignificant. But she keeps seeing his long gentle face in her mind and imagining that she might see him in the streets of the town. She wonders how he is coping for work and income. She remonstrates with herself to stop but the sense of a connection to him continues. She has not seen him since before Christmas. He refused to come indoors that day, despite the icy rain drops falling from his coat and hood.

'I came to apologise,' he repeated. 'I don't want to, but I will have to miss a month.'

'Robin, that doesn't matter. I am not bothered about the money. Do come in, you must be frozen.'

He was resolute, putting a Christmas card into her hand and hurrying away along the road.

'He will be drenched before he gets home,' she worried aloud, 'soaked through. That coat is too thin.'

Why didn't she stop him and give him a lift? She thought of this too late to act.

Now she gives each of the pavement dwellers anxious glances as she hurries past in case he might have sunk to join them. His situation could have become worse. She knows he lives in his mother's house, so he is unlikely to be homeless, but the thought that he might be in trouble, of whatever kind, keeps returning to her. That young girl was someone's daughter, once had a roof, a home.

The Big Issue seller outside the shopping centre is still there in all weathers, patiently standing with her bundle of magazines, being ignored by passers-by.

One day, she approaches the woman, careful to have her purse ready, intending to purchase the paper without conversation or eye contact. But she finds herself looking at her, the Romanian in her dark swaddling. She has a scarf wound around her head and her skirts reach to the ground, covering her shoes. There are layers of colours and materials but they are indistinct, serving only to obscure and insulate. Christine's own clothes are chosen to present herself, to display a fashion awareness, financial status, represent who she is.

The woman's face lightens as she approaches. Christine thinks she must be pleased to make a sale on a day when the weather is so foul. The woman nods, her eyes meeting Christine's; her smile is wide and reveals stained teeth. The hand she holds out for the money is brown and roughened.

The second time Christine stops to buy, she sees the woman sideways and realises that she is pregnant, unmistakably so. Unsure if the woman speaks English, she points to the swell in the long skirt with a question in her gesture that is understood.

'Yes, child, number three.' The woman grins showing all her teeth again. She gives Christine the look of complicity and resignation which women exchange, the look of shared knowledge, knowledge Christine does not, in fact, have. It is a shock to her that someone so far on in her pregnancy has to stand for hours in all weathers, hoping to make a living from meagre and unpopular sales. She smiles her sympathy and walks away thoughtfully.

Every time Christine nears the Riding Centre the woman calls out to her. Sometimes Christine is hurrying, unsure if she has enough change, but if the woman is there and sees her, she finds she must stop, buy the magazine and try to have a few words. 'How are you, how long will you be here today, are you seeing a doctor?' She has learnt from the woman's broken phrases that there are two other children are being cared for somewhere but it is not clear where.

'What about—the father?' she asks.

'Yes, he home.' The answer leaves her as mystified as before.

It is hard for her to imagine what life is for a mother who stands in all weathers on the street, trying to make what must be a miserable living. She wonders where the woman sleeps, where she has come from to stand in the chill grey, and why. A sense of inadequacy overtakes her if she ponders these questions. She takes the magazine home and puts it on a coffee table. Occasionally, she flicks to the pages where there are appeals for missing persons. My husband is missing, she thinks, but he wanted to go and I have to let him go.

She has stopped waiting for his return or any message. The silence has grown around her and she accepts it. If the phone rings the possibility of his voice hangs in the air and evaporates in an instant. Her colleagues have noticed the change. They are less solicitous, the air between them is warmer, looser. She feels their presence as a mist or a blanket, something soft, muffling pain, comforting anguish. She is a woman whose husband has chosen to leave her, missing but not lost. People know she is on her own, but she has told no-one the true story. She is a woman with a hole inside, into which her old self has been sucked down. Christine is a stranger, moving on lines, set out for her, aping the ways of her predecessor, but unknown.

She begins going out of town to shop in a new supermarket. The unfamiliar layout is curiously useful. It forces her to think because she has no idea what to buy. Her mind is blank. What do people who live alone buy for themselves? The first few times, she buys ready prepared meals with fancy names. She remembers her old cravings for pickled herrings and olives with potato salad, both of which Ray hated. She buys fruit, tomatoes, ham, crusty bread and wine. These make a meal she does not tire of. She thinks of herself as picnicking, keeping alive and passing an evening as bearably as possible. Sometimes it is interminable; she paces the house looking for something she does not want to find. Then she forces toast and milky tea on herself, longing for sleep, for the next day's routine to come as quickly as possible and also so slowly that it might not come at all. She goes to bed early with a book she hardly starts to read before dropping into deep, numbing sleep.

Chapter Ten

The year began with rain and it continues into the following month; wet dark day follows wet dark day. The trees behind the house are lines in the sky and the flower beds full of brown stalks and rotting leaves, the sodden debris of winter. The focus of news reports has shifted from the deaths of migrants at sea to the more comprehensible horror of flooded homes, broken bridges, cars stranded in swollen streams. The hospital is busy. Wet surfaces mean sudden falls and car crashes; more broken arms and smashed legs to mend.

The night when Ray left her she had been pleased he was going out. She did not want to say goodbye. She felt his presence as irritating, blocking her pleasures for the evening, simple as they were. Had she wished him gone, out of the house, away from her? The question keeps returning. Her satisfaction with their life, the smart clean lines of their house, the orderly progress of their days, the distance from the estate where she had grown up, the annual show of the garden, all these constructed a wall. She had thought she had achieved a safe, tidy life, visible to all as a success and, if there were ever bad dreams or intimations of emptiness, she had a wall to keep them out. Sometimes a gap did open and her safety was at risk. Always, always she closed it with cheerfulness, with practical planning, diverted herself with work and friendly conversations. But the wall has gone and emptiness yawns beneath her. The sense of purpose—to have a good life, to be happy, to be seen to be a successful couple—all these have evaporated, dissolved. He has taken away her own understanding of who she is. One morning she stands gazing at the cherry tree outside the living room window. Its branches are nearly touching the glass but it looks lifeless, a collection of sticks. Under the ground, the roots cling on, spreading out, gripping onto clay, reaching for the house itself.

'It is too large. It blocks the light in summer. It will have to come down.'

She feels this resolution is a mark of acceptance. Change has to come, will arrive, needs to be known as inevitable. The tree is too close to the house so it will have to come to the end of its life. A show of spring blossoms is a superficial and unnecessary symbol of success or status.

The walk to work is a struggle into a north easterly, blowing hail into her face and biting her nose. She goes up the street and across the cinder track towards the car park as quickly as she can. Entry into the stuffy medicated air of the main atrium is a relief. She shakes out her hair from her hood as she crosses the hall and goes along the corridor to the Physio Department. As she approaches Out Patients there is a confusion of people at the reception desk, holding out appointment letters and raising their voices. She lifts her eyebrows in query but the receptionist makes a negative gesture with both hands that Christine does not understand.

In the Department, staff are coming and going in the corridor without the usual sense of purpose. No patients have been allocated to the cubicles. The customary routine is in disarray. She goes into the staff room, to leave her bag and coat, to find Paveen with her back to her, looking out of the window.

'What on earth is going on? Everyone is in a muddle. The patients haven't even been started in the queue yet. There's people outside complaining.'

Paveen turns; her face is distorted and tears have left trails across her cheeks.

'Oh, my dear. What is wrong?'

Paveen takes her hands, holds them steadily and in a low voice, tells her that their Head of Department, Liz, is not coming into work because yesterday she returned, from a visit to their daughter at University, to find her husband had hanged himself. 'On a beam in the garage. Hanging there when she opened the door to put the car away. A man of fifty two. He must have been so unhappy, but to do that to her? Knowing she would find him.'

Before Christine can speak, a junior physio puts her head around the door.

'The list is sorted, I think. We have started.'

The chairs are filling with patients, some familiar faces who try to catch her eye, hoping for a greeting and perhaps to exclaim about the morning's delay. Everyone in the department is in shock, although their duties continue. Whispered asides are exchanged over a quick break, glances are passed, as if to keep themselves upright and active they need eye contact from those others who hold this dreadful knowledge.

Christine sees to her first three patients, smiling, asking questions, demonstrating movements, using her hands to soothe and strengthen. She is in a trance, moving like a machine on a track she cannot see but which is laid out for her.

The next patient is a middle aged man she knows well. He has had a hip replacement after years of pain and needed an extensive period of hydrotherapy, which Christine has supervised in the pool. Today he is waiting for an assessment of his progress, his eyes anxiously seeking hers. She nods at him briefly as she goes past his chair. She should turn left to collect his notes, but she is walking in the opposite direction, away from the clinic, towards X Ray. The corridor stretches ahead. A porter passes, chatting to the old lady slumped in the wheel chair he is pushing. She reaches the swing doors which lead outwards and she plunges into the icy air. Her head is spinning, her stomach is about to heave. Gulping hard breaths, she tries to calm the thump in her chest.

Paveen appears beside her.

'Chrissie, are you ok? I saw you leave. Come on, the clinic is nearly done. You've only got a couple more. It has upset everyone. We just have to get on with it. Come on, love, come in out of the cold, we can talk.'

'I can't. I am sick. Tell them that. Please, I'm really sorry but I've got to go. Say it is a bug. Anything. Please, please, Paveen.'

Her friend is baffled, stands back to stare at her, begins to remonstrate. But something in Christine's eyes stops her.

'Ok. Shall I bring your coat out here so you don't have to go back in?'

'Thank you.'

She is conscious of the cold while she waits, but can do nothing except stand, her arms crossed against her chest, her body shivering, her face rigid. When Paveen returns, she huddles into her coat and sets off, hardly speaking a goodbye. She makes her way home, not looking up, seeing only her feet and the rough cinders of the track before reaching the winter stained pavements, her hands thrust deep into the pockets of her coat. As she crosses on the road to her side, she stumbles, her feet unreliable. She regains balance and plunges on. In her mind, the image of a hanged man. His hideous, bloated face. A swinging figure in a domestic garage. A picture of lasting pain.

She comes into the house at last. The heating is off and she keeps her coat on. A cold fever has taken hold of her body, her hands shake and her head is bursting.

She knew her boss's husband as a pleasant figure at social events, usually quietly in the background. She knew of him by report—tales of holidays and birthdays and funny family incidents—but nothing to suggest he was depressed. She wonders if he left an explanation of his actions, a note to say sorry, a note to say why.

A torrent of grief swells in her chest and she breaks into sobbing. Another man has deserted. Inflicted that horrific loss onto her old colleague, a steady competent woman she has known for years. A mother as well as a wife. With a teenage daughter who now has had her life broken into pieces.

Ray had not had that courage to die as a statement of suffering. He had sneaked off into the night, vanished into thin air, become a ghost hovering about her, but never seen.

'He should have hung himself,' she cries out, 'there on that tree, in front of the house. Everyone could have seen what he had done. Done to me. Done to us.'

'Coward, filthy coward,' she rants, roaming the house back and forth, from room to room, as if movement will keep the agony from wrecking her.

Finally, she sinks onto a chair, still huddled in her coat. So it is over, she recognises. There was a marriage, a life. But that has gone. It was a sham, but I didn't see it. Perhaps I didn't want to see it, but he did. I am a woman without a husband. I shall tell everyone we have separated, for good. No more hiding and avoiding. Marriages end and people live on.

Poor Liz will never forget the hanging man. Whatever that man was suffering, however bad it seemed to him, his wife will never forgive him for leaving her with that horror in the garage, that violence which will last in her mind wherever she looks, whatever she does. Christine shrinks in her own mind from that picture. But can his wife ever forgive herself for not knowing, for not seeing his despair?

Tear soaked and weary, Christine curls up and lays her head on a cushion. 'If Ray comes back, when he comes back, he might ask for forgiveness. Could I forgive his plan, his secret absence?'

Out loud, she says, 'Whenever he comes back, our life is over. That's that.'

'But I am alive,' she whispers. 'My roots are clinging on.'

If Ray was suffering, he could have found other ways of letting her know. He had stayed his kindly, considerate self; she had thought him present in their life. But he must have been going away for a long time, in secret. Absenting himself in stages, by design, with intent. The silence was already there. Leaving that evening was the last step in the path he had chosen much earlier.

'Chrissie—are you ok? Text me back.'

The phone pings with Paveen's second message. Outside, rain clouds are racing over the roofs opposite, the newly budded trees bending in the wind. For hours during the night the wind has moaned along the street, chasing stray branches and threatening to topple bins. Christine stood by her living room window, curtains half open, and looked into the tumultuous darkness. Her limbs were stiff and she was conscious of her stomach growling. But it made no difference. The night passed as the day had, slowly, in silence, sitting slumped and tear-stained in a chair, or standing motionless at the window.

Day again, it is time for her shift to start. She cannot make herself fit into the morning routine. She has not eaten, drunk only water. She gives herself a little shake and reads Paveen's anxious messages. She must ring the department and say she is ill.

'I am sick,' she says. 'I am a sick person who knows nothing, who knew nothing about my marriage, knew nothing about the man I was married to. Perhaps he hated me. Or despised me, what I was, I am.

'Ray was safe for me. I married him because he was. Perhaps I was too safe for him.'

She remembers him saying the dervish dancers had ecstasy. She thinks of the solemn whirling figures enacting their formal ritual, each enclosed in his own self, his own mind. Has he gone on a search for experiences he could never have with her, never have as a couple? She was silent with him, so many times was quiet rather than shake the safe roots.

She stops to look in the hall mirror. Her hair is bedraggled, as if she has been in the wind, still banging about outside in the world. She has always been secretly proud of her shiny cap of hair. 'My little blondie.' Had Ray really called her that once, spoken to her with that tenderness, with so much sweetness? She grimaces at her reflection. How could he leave her so?

Turning away, she goes into the kitchen. With a new energy from the anger coursing through her body, she begins cleaning. She wipes and scrubs and washes, every object, every surface. The room fills with the smell of bleach and wet cloths. On the window sill, the phone bleeps again and then again. Her ears and eyes have closed to any reality but this, the need to be rid of every speck of dirt and dust as if she can, at the same time, wipe out the past.

Much later she rings the hospital to make her apologies. To ring in late is a staff sin, frowned on by the department seniors, because staffing levels are too low, no-one is free to pick up another's work. If Liz was at work, she would possibly face a telling off or a formal reprimand. But clearly everything is still in a crisis mode at the hospital, as in her life. Her message is taken without comment. She has a virus, must not give it to others, she will be back by the end of the week. She knows Paveen will ring as soon as she has a break in her shift and she waits.

'Chrissie. Did you get my texts this morning? How are you?'

'Sorry. I have been in bed and the phone was off. I slept through. That's why I didn't ring in time.'

'Let me bring you something after work. I could drop off a meal, soup, whatever you fancy.'

'No, thanks, Paveen. Really, I am better off just sleeping. I'll be ok. It is just a virus. It'll pass.'

The lie is easy to tell. The truth would be too difficult.

Time moves so heavily. She wonders how her mother, old, alone, with few interests, bears this terrible monotony of minutes. How does anyone bear the drag of the hours, the slow forward pull of each day's light. She eats toast, drinks tea, sits in silence or sleeps where she sits. At night she curls into the single bed in the spare room because the bed she shared with Ray is an accusation. When Friday arrives, and three days have passed in interminable slowness, she wakes early, dresses for work and walks briskly up the hill to be there on time.

Chapter Eleven

Christine ignores Gillian's phone call as she is on shift, but feels obliged later to listen to the message she has left. Gillian's voice is insistent; she is almost shouting.

'Ring me as soon as you get this. Ring me straight away.' She stands in the staff common room, casting a smile at a colleague who bustles in and sinks into a chair, sighing heavily.

'What a day! My feet are killing me. And one more miserable parent who won't help with their kid's exercises will finish me off. My face hurts from keeping quiet. I'll be glad when it is home time.'

'Yes,' she agrees. 'Me too.'

The phone is still in her hand. She has a few minutes of her break. She makes a swift decision to text Gillian and say she is at work and cannot ring until the evening. Whatever the problem, it can wait. As she starts phrasing the message, the phone rings again.

'Hi Gillian. I am sorry but I can't use my phone at work.'

'Chrissie. I have seen Ray. I saw him in town. This morning.'

The room swims. She can hear nothing, though she knows Gillian is still talking. Her colleague gets up to put the kettle on and glances at her. 'Hey, you ok?' Mute, Christine nods and swipes the phone off. She leaves the room, goes back to her list in the clinic before she starts a ward round, the words repeating in her head. Gillian has seen Ray. He is here. He is here.

It is impossible to go home at the end of her shift as if it is a routine day. She starts to walk past the end of Westfield Centre towards home, but turns towards the town. The days are lengthening into Spring and the late afternoon air is refreshing after the closed heat of the hospital.

Perhaps Gillian had made a mistake; perhaps it was not him. It is easy to see similarities from behind. Ray's back view is not distinctive. Except to me, she thinks. I could never mistake his curls, faded and thinner, but still his hair and only his hair; I could never be wrong if I saw the back of his head.

She walks without thought for where she is going, but her eyes search for every head, every face, every figure seen at a distance. She cannot see him. She stops in a bar on Northgate, a tapas plus wine bar place where the narrow strip of tables on the pavement are always full, but which she has never entered. She makes a show of studying the menu, orders a glass of wine, olives and bread. The bar is quiet but a stream of early drinkers is beginning to take tables, groups of three and four, young working people or older women, a few men in office gear. There is a reserved sign on one long table, set aside, she expects, for a large party—perhaps a birthday or work outing? Christine looks around, noticing how the women who have been at work are dressed, short black skirts and heeled boots. They have shiny hard looking nails, talons glued on to immaculate hands. Her own hands are plain but, she thinks, serviceable, ready for work. How do they manage to do anything she wonders. Do they scratch their lovers with those claws? This thought is startling. She draws her coat closer around her despite the warmth of the bar, conscious of her white uniform being visible and shuffles her heavy black work shoes out of sight under the table.

The refrain in her head goes on and on. Ray is here. He is somewhere here. After the first glass is empty, she signals to the girl who served her and orders another. It is a deep red and the tannin hits her roof of her mouth. She is the only person sitting alone, but no one notices her. At last, a little unsteadily, she pays and leaves. As she walks home, she turns the phone back on. In minutes it rings.

'Where are you, Chrissie? I am outside your house.'

'Gillian, I am out tonight. Please tell me now what happened.'

'I want to see you, Chrissie. Please come home.' She is silent.

'Well, I just saw the back of his head in Morrisons. I ran towards him, I called out his name, but he didn't hear me, or didn't want to hear me. By the time I got through checkout, I was at the till when I saw him, he had gone. It was about three this afternoon. I finished work early today, was just picking up some fish…'

'Chrissie? Are you still there? Did you hear me?'

She swipes the call off while Gillian is still talking. She turns and goes back along the street in the direction of the city centre. She goes towards Harry's, the real ale place where Ray would go on his weekly nights out. Her chest tightens, making her hurry; she puts her head down and walks faster. He might be there tonight. If he was at the supermarket earlier, he might be there now, having a pint, on his own or with friends. He might be meeting someone. Since that night, so many months ago, when she woke to the sound of the phone and there was only silence, Christine has never considered that her husband might have gone off with another woman. She did check his phone for texts or strange numbers in the early days, but found nothing, only contacts she recognised, messages arranging a beer or work meetings. Now she is frightened to think she could see him with an unfamiliar face, in an unknown situation; she might see a stranger, a woman, with him.

As she enters the small space of the pub, she hesitates with the thump of her heart filling her ears. Perhaps she is about to see him at last. She has to push past drinkers clustered around the bar. There are only few empty seats along the wooden panels of the room but a searching glance reveals that Ray is not there. Desperate weakness overtakes her. Where is he? How can she go on, an abandoned woman?

Nobody looks up, nobody notices a woman on her own in a crowded pub. Ray, please come in, talk to me, find me again. Her hand is shaking as she takes her drink to sit by the window, where she can see the whole room and whoever comes in. Some of the afterwork people are moving on, leaving froth stained glasses, saying their goodbyes, but new groups are coming in, smartly dressed for a night out. The other seats at her table are in demand and soon a couple indicate they would like to sit alongside her. She nods agreement. The level in the glass of wine sinks. She wants to get up for another, but realises she is unsteady. She has eaten nothing substantial for hours and the wine is infusing her limbs and head with heaviness. Ray has not appeared. She must stop expecting him. The hope that was so painfully lodged in her chest dissolves. The man and woman at her table are deep into their conversation.

'I blame the parents,' insists the woman.

Her companion shakes his head emphatically. 'It's the small uns. They are worse than the big uns.'

'We don't let our Chloe do that. She knows better.'

'Mebbe not but I tell thee, it's the small uns who leave all that rubbish there. Doesn't matter what the council says it'll do, it never gets done.'

It seems they can both agree about this and they look encouragingly at Christine to include her in this summary of the problem. 'The council does nothing', they both nod at her with knowing smiles. The man grunts, keeping one hand firmly on his glass, and the woman gives a patient sigh. Christine tries to smile back, although she would really hate to agree with them. She thinks she must get up and go home. A new idea occurs. Ray trusted his colleague, Brenda. Christine has met her several times. She is from a Polish family, a generous person. Someone who deals calmly with trouble and difficulty. Christine will ring Brenda to find out if she knows where he is today.

A man sways out from his place at the bar and holds out his arm as she makes for the door.

'Hey, steady on. Does tha need a hand, love? More than a hand maybe? Is that a uniform I see on the little woman?'

She can rouse herself enough to shake him off, but she will not be able to make the walk home. Taxis in this city are plentiful and cheap, lined up waiting at this time of the evening for the drinkers to give up and go home. The Pakistani drivers are quiet and philosophical about the drunks. Some will still be here in the early hours. Christine pays and stumbles into the house with as much dignity as she can.

Ray's phone is on the kitchen window ledge where it has been for weeks. She finds the number for Brenda and her finger hovers over the ring button. Then she looks at it. She stops. If this colleague knows Ray's whereabouts, she will also know where and why he went. She might also know that he went without a message for his wife, left her with silence. A silence that began months or years ago seeping into their life, the life she, Christine, had protected from noise. A quiet life. She cannot talk to someone who might know and admit that she does not know. She has been hiding from that conversation since the first night. How embarrassing would it be for Brenda? She cannot do that to someone so kind. How humiliating for them both if she did.

What difference can it make? If he is back in town, he has not come to see me. He does not want to see me or for me to see him. He is still silent. And I am still alone. It is a mystery what has happened. A mystery no-one could unfold or explain to me. Perhaps no-one can explain it to him. The dusk has deepened outside the kitchen window. She steps out into the garden. The first signs of Spring growth have begun; pale shoots gleam along the borders. She stands under the acer tree and looks up. Tiny curls of new leaf are visible on each branch. Through its limbs, she can see a faint glow of stars. There is comfort in the company of trees, she thinks. Comfort and calm enter her and she stands quietly in the garden as the night comes on.

Chapter Twelve

'Chrissie, come in for a coffee. Take a break.' Paveen has caught her sleeve as they pass in the corridor.

Christine follows her into the overcrowded staff room, which is full of lockers with too few chairs and only one table. They had been promised better facilities in the new hospital but this room has a familiar smell of shoes and disinfectant and the usual shortage of space. 'Sorry to be so blunt, but as my family will tell you, I can't help straight speaking. I am a bit worried about you. You're not looking so good, love, you know.'

Paveen spreads her hands in a gesture both inviting and instructional. Outside it is a still day with no wind under a heavy sky. The season is turning too slowly.

'It is this time of year. It is the weather; it gets you down, doesn't it?'

Paveen puts a mug into her hand, shaking her head. 'You seem cut off. I know it hasn't been good with you and Ray. But has something happened? Has he come back? And the horrible business with Liz's husband upset you, I know it hit you hard.'

Christine cannot meet her eyes. She fixes her gaze on the mug. It is inscribed in blue and gold lettering, 'Royal Wedding Greetings'.

'You haven't been out on staff nights, haven't come round when I've asked you. The Taliban are not that bad.'

Christine looks up.

'That's what me and my sisters call our brothers. They are not really bad, just bossy.'

'Anyway,' she grins, 'we're Sikh, remember?' They both laugh.

'Paveen, I can't talk in here.' Christine is anxious about the door opening on a colleague. The walls of the room are closing in on her.

'Of course not. But will you come over to ours, tonight, say, straight after work? Mum will be disgustingly keen to meet you and fuss like nobody's business, but we will be able to get

73

some peace. I shall demand it. And it is quieter than here, well, some of the time anyway.'

As Christine comes into the narrow hallway of the Victorian terrace where Paveen lives with her family, she carefully takes off her shoes and puts them with the others in a line against the wall. The row of hooks on the wall for coats is overflowing but Paveen insists on taking her jacket to lay in a back room. Paveen has changed out of her uniform into a green sheath dress, embroidered at the hem in darker colours with white touches, over loose trousers falling into narrow ankle cuffs. A fine scarf in a lighter shade is wound around her neck. Christine realises she has never seen her in her home environment, dressed like this. She looks relaxed and beautiful, with her thick dark hair falling smoothly down her back.

The front room is full of colour and texture. She sees low sofas, cushions on the floor, rugs and embroidered hangings. It is comfortable and enclosing. She sinks into a chair, involuntarily smiling. A tray of tea with tiny cups appears, brought in by a skinny girl in high heels and short tight cut jeans; behind, an older woman comes with another tray set out with plates of samosas, sweet golden pastries plus milk chocolate digestives. 'This is my sister,' Paveen introduces. 'Oh, and this is Mum.'

The introductions take several minutes. Paveen's mother holds out a hand and grasps Christine's firmly. 'So glad to see you.' Her smile is direct and warm. 'Paveen tells us what a good colleague you are.'

'Yeah,' says the sister, 'right on.'

'She is doing engineering at college, can you believe?' Paveen grins at this fashion plate who sticks a tongue at her.

There is giggling behind the door and two small children tumble in, a boy and girl of similar ages.

'Bad luck,' Paveen says, 'here are the twins.'

Christine does not like to ask who is their mother. She concentrates on engaging with the boy, who offers her the samosas and stands waiting for her to take a bite and exclaim how delicious they are. But everyone is ushered out by Paveen calling out in her clear high tones, 'Privacy.'

Nodding and smiling, the family clears the room, in stages. The mother is last, continuing to ask if there is anything else Christine would perhaps like to eat until the door closes behind her.

'You see,' Paveen says, 'you have to shout here, or there is never any peace. At least the brothers are still at work or we would never be left alone.'

'You look lovely,' Christine says.

'Yeah, but too old,' she shrugs.

'Hardly too old! Are you thirty?'

'Thirty five. Yes, that's too old to be single, and too old to get a husband, though they keep trying.'

'Is there anyone?'

'There was. But you know, it is hard if it is not in the family, the faith, even if we don't really keep the faith.' Paveen rolls her eyes. 'Anyway it didn't work out. Now Mum probably wouldn't care if he was a Martian, green face and all, just to get me married off. I think I am fine as I am now. Who needs a Martian anyway?'

Christine begins to laugh with her but suddenly cannot speak. Paveen leans forward and offers her a paper hankie. 'You look as if you could cry.'

Tears have already fallen down her cheeks. She sits with face down, wipes her cheeks and blows her noise and still they fall. The smell of spices and pastry rise from the samosa; she has only taken one bite. Paveen quietly removes the plate from her knee to a table.

At last she can speak, her voice croaky in the soft air of the room. She lifts her head to tell Paveen, the first time she has told anyone, the story that started with a phone call in the night. The mysterious disappearance of her husband and her life. That he had planned to leave without any message. That sometimes she thinks him a coward and hates him; sometimes she is full of guilt that she wanted him gone even if she did not know it. She talks on and on, saying things she had not intended.

Paveen listens, leaning forward to catch every word, her small face creased with concern. Christine takes a soggy breath and stops, her head up.

'You see, he is not a missing person. He is an absent one. By his choice. And he plans, it seems, to come back at the end of the year, in a few months perhaps, who knows. I don't, Paveen. I have no idea. But perhaps he just couldn't tell me.'

'Despicable man to do that to you.' And, 'What courage, woman. Go, Christine. All these months and you have coped with this.' Paveen's voice is clear and fierce.

She stands and draws her into a hug. Christine is conscious of the slippery material of Paveen's dress on her neck. She can smell a faint aroma of food and a musky perfume. She imagines the hallway filled with all the family waiting to see what was happening. But she relaxes as the hug goes on and returns it with a pink glow of warmth and gratitude.

Chapter Thirteen

Later that evening, walking home after she and Paveen have said goodbye, swinging her arms, Christine feels a loosening deep inside. She is nearly halfway through a century of years: she is strong, professional, able, free. Paveen's indignation was a cleansing force sweeping through her, bones and blood. The drinkers have started to emerge; groups of threes and fours, no coats even though the Spring air is still cold, the girls with bare legs. When she was their age she was one of the crowd: dancing, picking up boys.

'But,' she thinks, 'I was always the careful one, not going too far, staying at the edge of everything, my mother's voice always warning me against too much fun, not to let go. Oh yes, I was a careful one. Ray was the careful choice as I went into my thirties, after lost love and dreary outings with men who bored me. He was clever, interested in me, always thoughtful. But what was he thinking? I had no idea.'

She remembers the first time she saw him, when she was waiting at the reception desk of the College, nervous but determined, wanting to ask about the course she had seen in the brochure, ready to take the first step towards a new life. The boy and girl ahead in the queue were relaxed and confident of their right to be in this place, while her heart was pumping too quickly. She had asked her boss for a morning off without saying she was thinking of retraining, of leaving the office work she was competent at and bored with. A man came briskly down the hallway, carrying papers. Someone who worked here. He passed her and gave her a sideways glance. That was all, just a sympathetic look as if he knew she was so uncertain and he was giving encouragement. An ordinary-looking man, a little older than her, wearing the kind of clothes she expected to see a lecturer in, casual trousers and a corduroy jacket, a man with kind eyes. She straightened her back and stepped forward to speak to one of the women behind the desk.

A week later she was coming through the swing doors when she saw him in the corridor with a young student. Could she thank him for that silent assistance? Before she could decide, he turned from the boy he had been talking to, smiled and spoke.

'Hello again. You did sign up then. What are you planning to do?'

'I am going to do an Access course this September. I am going to see the tutor now about a reading list.'

'I have taught on that course. Not going to teach on it this year, unfortunately.' He smiled. Christine was entitled to study, could talk to tutors, was someone who was going to college.

'I would like to train as a physiotherapist, if I can, that is. I have always been interested in medical things, well, that kind of work. I liked biology at school. I know it is a long course,. I have read up about it.'

Her mother has been scathing about the idea.

'What on earth is the point of spending all that time studying again? You've got a good job. You should be grateful. It is a husband you need and you won't get one buried in books. You are not so clever as you think, my girl. You don't want to step out of where you belong.'

'It is great to have a goal like that. And being a physio is an excellent profession.' The man called Ray nodded at her and offered to show her where the course room was on the first floor.

That was the beginning. A slow movement of smiles and interested eyes; an invitation to the pub one evening after classes; a quiet understanding that this would be a regular occasion. She could tell him about the topic they had covered, chat about the other students, a mixture of nineteen year olds who had failed at school plus five older people like her, grabbing another chance with more enthusiasm than the young. He suggested outings to galleries, plays, the latest film. For months, they hardly touched, kissed only lightly when saying hello or goodbye. Walking through the town, she thinks how proud she was to do those things with him: I was training for a profession and I had a professional boyfriend who knew about culture. We were good company. He supported me all through my studies. Waited for me when I went away for the course. After months had passed, he asked me to come to his flat and we made love in his single bed in the same kind, slow way we became friends. We bought a house when I had qualified, because we could; making excuses to my mother was impossible after a while.

'Where are you going, miss? When are you going to be home? Stopping out again, are you? No shame. Is he going to make an honest woman of you?' She had wanted to laugh sometimes, or shout back.

The marriage was inevitable. She could not say when it was agreed or how. Pretence—the word came into her head. Had she ever felt happy, loving, anything more than secure? Had she been pretending emotions for the sake of safety and comfort? Her mind encountered a new and terrible idea, that perhas they had both been pretending.

Getting married settled her mother—she was fond of saying to the neighbours, 'A Lecturer!' Respectability was restored and Ray became a favourite. He could charm her in those days, because of his job, middle-classness, gentle ways. But it is a long time since he even visited her mother. Another absence. As she walks along, Christine looks steadfastly into her past. It comes to her as a certainty that she did not pretend in the beginning. It had been love, a kind friendly love which has dissolved, gone, left her behind.

She looks for Robin among the people drifting along past the bars and clubs. She wonders if he ever comes into town, if he has friends to meet and buy a drink for. He has no money to spare but perhaps he can manage an occcassional beer. She does have Robin's address; she had asked for it so she could post him a card at Christmas. She walks through the crowded bus station, as a short cut home, and decides to visit him the next day. It is a step over an invisible line but the idea, once formed, is an unmistakable resolution.

It is clearly an ex-council house, the poorer sort built in a later decade with cheap bricks and a mean cramped look—it is half the size of her mother's house which was built immediately post war, broad fronted and generous.

She is nervous. Perhaps he will mind this intrusion, will think she is chasing the money still owed. The front garden is a square of grass edged by neglected beds, with last year's weeds showing green shoots. She knocks, then sees a bell and rings it too.

It is a narrow room off a tiny hall with the small kitchen visible at the end. A sagging sofa takes up one wall and opposite are crowded bookshelves on either side of a cheap wooden fire surround by a gas fire. Against that side of the room are stacked bin bags and cardboard boxes. Clothes spill out of some, others bulge with hardware so that the plastic is stretched and thin. Each box contains more books. There is a smell of dust and cleaning fluid. Robin hops from one foot to another, his eagerness flowing through his limbs and sending his arms waving out to the side.

'I wondered how you are as I haven't seen you. Sorry, I should have asked before I came if it was ok.'

He moves papers and magazines to clear a space for her to sit, gesturing at the same time at the piles of stuff along the wall.

'I'm just busy with all this. At last. I am having a sort out. Sorry about the debt—I haven't forgotten. I am going to pay you it all. But how are you? Have you heard anything from, you know, your husband?'

She shakes her head.

They both look at the piles of bags and boxes.

'Is this all your mother's stuff?' she asks, conscious of the need to tread delicately.

'Some of it's my brother's, but mostly Mum's. People told me to clear it out ages ago. I am just getting round to it.'

'She had a lot of books,' she points to the shelves.

'She read and read. The library staff all knew her really well. She was always in there. She read to us as kids, to some of our friends too. Those are her favourites. Mine too. It was one of the few things she could do in the last years. When the pain was bad.'

'What was her name?'

'Ruth—it's a Biblical name, you know. It means companion, a beautiful person. She loved history, local history especially. She was quite an expert, uncovered things the Civic Society hadn't known. Even found out about a composer who lived here and was killed in the First World War. There is a blue plaque on his family house because of my mother and her research.'

'It must be hard, doing all this. Letting it all go.'

He nods.

'What is the plan? What are you going to do with it all?'

'Charity shops if I can get it there. Bit by bit.'

Then he rushes into the kitchen to fill a kettle, leaving her gazing at the task he set himself. She can see a scuffed table and plastic chair. His mother died six years ago and only now is he able to get rid of these traces of her, the detritus of a life lost.

She has made no effort to change anything in her house, waiting in limbo, with Ray's carefully stored collection of vinyl records, his books and papers all around her.

As he hands her a mug, she asks, 'Can I help?'

Startled, he hesitates, but only for a second. He grins.

'Thank you, Christine.'

'Call me Chrissie—all my friends do.' She smiles. 'No time like the present, as they say. Come on then.'

Christine is wearing a pale grey sweater and smart black trousers. All washable, she reminds herself, as she heaves the first bag to one side. These clothes smell musty as she tips them out, but the skirt and blouse she holds up are clean. Plain workable, sensible clothes, nothing expensive or fancy, no fashionable garments from any era. She sees his mother before them; Ruth, a thoughtful, practical woman, not slim but not fat, not tall but not petite, an ordinary person with work-stained hands and short grey hair she cuts herself. There is no extravagance in these markers of a woman's life.

Only the books show a richness, an abundance of interest, an expansion of mind and heart into other worlds: classic novels, modern fiction of all kinds, travel books with glossy photos—these, Christine surmises, given to her as gifts—history compilations and special studies. Plus books about Warmfield city and its history, books about trains and mines and building and the changes in people's lives. There are lots of garden books, mostly manuals about growing fruit and vegetables. On the shelves, Robin has kept what he knew were her favourites, the Brontës and all of Austen, Dickens, Doris Lessing and Jane Smiley, too, paperbacks carefully kept. Christine runs her finger along the spines. Some of these are titles she read herself when the excitement of her new studies had opened up new worlds, new pleasures. She had gained the confidence to browse in the library, to look around at the the glossy displays in the book shop even without buying a book that time. She was someone who read literary books. It is a while now since she has read fiction. She wonders why.

After an hour sorting, discussing and deciding, Christine begs a rest. Robin rushes anxiously to make tea again. She leans back on the sofa to consider.

'You could make some money out of all this,' she suggests. 'Ebay for the kitchen stuff, all those pyrex dishes for instance. The mincer would sell too, unless you are going to use it? The books could go to that antique book shop, you know the one, yes? That man who runs it is nice, an expert, he would be interested to give you a price and he might even come here to look at them.'

She wonders if she has strayed too far, trodden too much over the border. 'Busy women are the worst.' Who said that? Ray, of course.

Robin perches on a stool and chews his nails. His hair falls softly over his forehead from a high peak. He brushes it back.

'Your mother would want you to benefit. Especially as times are hard.'

He gives his jerky nod. In the silence a car parks noisily on the pavement next door.

She notices a keyboard poking out from under the one chair in the room. 'What's that? Is that something else to sell? A music thing?

He leans and pulls it out.

'I can't sell this,' he says. 'It's mine, I play it, I play it a lot.'

'What kind of music?' she asks, trying not to show her surprise to this young man who keeps surprising her.

'Classical, mostly anyway. And some stuff I compose for myself.'

She nods as if this is entirely clear to her.

'How interesting.'

'Come on then. Let's divide into what will sell and what can be given away.'

She is conscious of his gentle physical presence as they work, his long pony face turned towards her in query or agreement. She has an urge to put her arms around him, to stroke his forehead smooth, to touch his long fingers. The impulse is so strong that she has to move, picking up bags and taking them to the door.

'I'll take these outside and put them in my car now,' she says over her shoulder. 'Then I can drop them off at the Hospice shop any time I'm passing.'

Outside as she opens the boot, she wonders at her thoughts. She had wanted in those seconds to take him into her arms, like a lover, to be caressed gently but intently. She feels not shame, but something else. He is too young for her, but not so young that it is impossible. If I were one of those cougar women, a predatory female, perhaps I could entice him, I could enchant him. Ridiculous, of course.

At least the sap is rising, she thinks. I am not completely wizened, dried up. Light hearted, she goes back to their task. Robin notices her cheerfulness and slowly it infuses him too. He stops less frequently to examine an item, to pause over its significance, struggle to assign it to a future. By the time the day is darkening, they have cleared a considerable space in the room, with boxes of books and kitchen equipment neatly arrayed by the window.

'How many rooms have you got?'

'Just two bedrooms, plus a tiny one like a cupboard.'

'You could have a lodger, then. Take someone in who needs a place, even a refugee. Get a little money for it.'

'Who would want to live here? There's only one bathroom and one kitchen.'

'The question is, could you share? If it brought you rent? You could choose who, make sure it is someone you like, who likes the same things as you. Books for instance. Music. You like classical music, you have lots of CDs over there and you play.'

She hesitates as she finishes this sentence. She does not understand about his music. The poverty of the house and his situation do not suggest extensive piano lessons as a child and he has said nothing about this when talking of his mother's support for him and his brother. But she is so convinced that she has had a brilliant idea to help him that she has a new burst of energy. While he is still pondering her suggestion and apologising that he has not given her anything to eat, she looks for her coat and beckons him to the door.

'Fish and chips. We have earned it. My treat.'

He hangs back, shaking his head.

'Thanks, but no, I can't.'

'Yes, you can. So can I.' Christine laughs. 'Come on.'

'The chippie is just around the corner. If you insist, Chrissie.' It is the first time he has used her name like that.

'We are going to the proper place. We are going to The Whaler for a sit down. We have earned it.'

Sitting opposite him in the restaurant, she is conscious of their difference, that she is eating here with a young man she hardly knows, who is wearing a shirt with a worn collar and trainers that are past mending. She smiles encouragingly as she can see he is also uncomfortable, taking quick glances around at the tables full of families and couples. The smell of hot fat fills the room. The food, enormous slabs of fish in crisp batter, golden piles of chips, thin sliced white and brown bread, two pots of tea, cheers them both. In companionable silence, they eat. Finally, Christine pushes her plate away.

'Enough. Not another chip!'

He grins and carries on until his plate is cleared. Relaxed, he begins to tell her about his Christmas at the hospice, how many relatives came and how upbeat the atmosphere was against the odds, despite the pain and distress in every room. He tells her he has begun to feel better about his mother's time there, to see that the medical staff had to take control and make decisions, even though it still pains him to remember.

Christine squirms, listening and looking steadily into his eyes but inwardly full of guilt. She told her mother she was going to volunteer for the day and she had intended to. He had inspired her with the idea. She left her mother on Christmas Day for a supposed good deed but, in fact, she did not go. She curled up in front of a film on the television, ate chocolates until the sweetness disgusted her, drank her way down a bottle of wine and then another. She had asserted her right to do exactly as she pleased, but the result was only drunkenness and sorrow. She thinks for a second of telling this to Robin but his innocence stops her.

'Time to go home. Think about the lodger idea. Won't you?'

As she drops him off at his house, he stands by the car door for a moment, then crosses to the car window and gives her a wave and one of his jerky smiles.

'Goodnight, Chrissie. You are a good friend.'

Chapter Fourteen

The letter is in a drawer in the hall table. She put it there immediately, unopened. Before she picked it up from the mat, she knew his handwriting. It is an A4 brown envelope, containing more than one sheet of paper, addressed in his tiny script.

It arrived on a working day, waiting for her as she came home from the hospital, a mild breeze blowing up behind her and lifting the collection of the day's post before she shut the door. The postmark is visible, but smudged, the stamp an ordinary English one.

It has stayed in the drawer for several days. With deliberate care, she ignores it, passes through the hall by walking as far from the edge of the table as possible. She has told no one that it has come.

Today the world is bursting with growth. Although the air is brisk, the earth is sending out tendrils and shoots; daffodils colour the banks of roadsides and fill the park; the trees are sparkling with new leaves of translucent green. The cherry tree in front of Christine's house is beginning to break out in exuberant pink.

She smiles at it as she stands there to use her phone. You have escaped another year, she tells it silently, you have won me over again.

'Rob, it's Chrissie. Are you still free today?'

She puts the phone down on the window sill and carelessly leaves it. Robin is coming for coffee and to show her the new tune. He will carry his keyboard on the bus and walk up from the station to be here in half an hour.

Perhaps she will be able to persuade him to stay for lunch. He is a fussy eater, but the new recipe for leek soup is delicious so if she leaves it simmering, he might be tempted by the warm vegetable aroma. She begins to clear the chopping board and vegetable trimmings, wiping surfaces, humming as she works. The phone rings but she has forgotten where it is. With wet hands in the air, she rushes from room to room. When she finds it, there is a message from Gillian.

'Hi, Chrissie. I'm in town. Will pop in shortly.'

Christine swears lightly and, for a second, intends to ring back and cancel her friend's visit.

'What harm can it do? She won't stay long once she sees he is here. In any case, he is my friend too.' She remembers the last conversation with Gillian about Robin; her friend's studied concern—'Isn't he a bit young? I hope you are not, well… Chrissie, are you?' It still amuses her. Does Gillian think she is a cougar? 'There is not one pattern for friendship,' had been her cryptic reply, surprising them both.

She is convinced not to put Gillian off. Or she decides to take the risk of her meeting Robin here. It is unclear, but she goes back to her hum.

Robin arrives first. He is sporting a beard. He has shaved his soft floppy mop of hair into fashionable stubble. It makes him look older and tougher. His keyboard is housed in a long sports bag, which he stows carefully in the front room before joining Christine.

'This kitchen smells good.'

'They say the smell of coffee is tempting even to those who don't drink it. And that is leek and potato soup on the go too. Shall we have this drink first, Rob? How you are getting on with the house share? You can tell me how your week has been.'

'And you can tell me about yours, Chrissie.'

Companionably they sit at the table, drink the coffee, chat about events. The election is looming, dominating the news. It is of surprisingly little interest to Robin, who takes a lofty philosophical approach to current affairs, and Christine thinks it is her responsibility to encourage him to think about it differently. He has a friend living with him now and knows she is always keen to learn how they are managing.

When the doorbell goes, she remembers with a jolt that Gillian is expected. It is several weeks since they saw each other. In the hallway, Gillian is effusive, hugging Christine, exclaiming how good it is to see her, how well she is looking. Christine works hard to respond with similar warmth and leads her into the kitchen.

'Oh, hello. I didn't realise, sorry, I didn't know.'

Robin rises smoothly, holds out his hand and introduces himself, reminding her gently that they have met before.

Gillian takes the hand, her eyes wide, and with cheerful determination, sits. She glances around the room, seeing the flowers on the window sill, the new cookery book open on the side, the bright splash of a new print on the wall. There are tulips, with their scarlet and gold heads opening to flow over the lip of a glass vase. On the hall table, visible from her chair, she sees a pile of novels. She notices that Ray's music player has gone. She cannot stop herself turning her head to look back into the hall for other signs of change.

'How are things, Chrissie? Have you heard anything?' This with a sideways glance at Robin and a raised eyebrow.

Christine knows her friend wants to talk about her situation, but that she is also torn between discretion in front of Robin and the urgency of her curiosity. 'You have chosen a good day to come,' she says casually. 'My friend Robin is going to play a new tune he has composed.' Robin smiles with faint embarrassment.

'He is something of a genius, you know. Oh yes, he is. I am making him blush but it is true. How many people could teach themselves to play classical piano music without a piano?'

Despite herself, Gillian is surprised and intrigued.

'He just taught himself in his head, didn't you? I can't even play a recorder, but while he was at school, he listened to lots of Mozart and Bach and worked out how some pieces could be played on a keyboard. Imagine that.'

'The school did get a shock,' Robin grins. 'You see, I asked if I could use the piano in the school hall one lunchtime. I wanted to see if I was right, if I could do it. I had got the sheet music for Bach's Two-part and Three-part Inventions and had learnt them and then added on some bits for myself. The teachers came running out and the music teacher, it was funny, he just kept asking me how many lessons I had had.'

'Robin's mother couldn't afford a piano, you see, so he taught himself. In his head.'

'They gave me lessons for a while after that, in free lunch breaks, but actually the teacher hadn't got much to show me. He was better at singing, choral stuff. He wasn't an expert.

You can't blame him. If he had been, he probably wouldn't have been teaching at our school.'

'So you really are a genius,' Gillian exclaims.

'No, it's whatever you really like, isn't it? You follow it through.'

'Do you play professionally?'

'No, no chance of that. I am too old. I play for myself. And I compose for fun.'

'What a waste! Have you got a job? Young man, you must get yourself into a proper orchestra, pursue a career.' Her voice is too loud in the quiet house.

Christine can see Robin is beginning to writhe under Gillian's insistence.

'You can hear him yourself. He has a keyboard and he is going to play for me, for us, now.'

'Are you working?' Gillian is determined.

'On and off.'

'Oh, I see. Chrissie, before we do listen, can I have a word, privately? I do want to hear what is happening?' Gillian has half risen out of her chair, demanding attention, asserting her right to intervene, to be the one who knows.

Christine raises each coffee cup into the air, letting the dregs fall into the sink with a rush. She stands there with her back to the room and grips the edge of the kitchen surface.

'Chrissie, are you ok?' Robin looks anxiously across the room at her.

'Has something happened?'

She turns to face them both.

'Yes. In fact, a letter has arrived. It is from Ray. I think it will be his explanation. Perhaps his excuses. Perhaps his demands. Who knows?'

'Why don't you know? You are not telling me you haven't opened it?'

'Robin, please play us the tune, the new one. I am looking forward to hearing it. You know, Gillian, I have heard a few now and I really think Robin could send them to a music publisher—or whatever happens nowadays.'

'But if he just wants to make music for himself, that is his business.' Robin looks at her carefully, checking her face. He gives her a grin of thanks, lopes off into the living room to set up his keyboard.

Gillian looks at her friend in bewilderment.

'I can't believe you don't want to open the letter. You must want to know what he is doing, why he has done what he has. You've got to open it.'

Christine thinks of the letter, lying in the drawer, folded brown paper holding more paper, with words waiting for her, waiting to explode. If they had arrived earlier, how she would have torn open that paper, eaten those words off the page with her hunger for answers.

'It makes no difference. Well, some in practical terms as we have to sort out the house, money etc. But whatever he has to say, whatever the explanation, it is done. I've put lots of his stuff in boxes upstairs. I was fed up with it all over the house.'

She thinks of how Spring has opened up the world outside, the birds busy in their nests, new life starting. The sabbatical year is more than half way through. September will come. On the cathedral spire in the city, the peregrine falcons are back, high above the shoppers, nurturing their young for the future and casting cold eyes on the life below.

Whenever she reads Ray's words, she will now be ready.

'What if he has, I don't know, had some kind of experience, like a mini breakdown, now he wants to come back, to be here again, with you, Chrissie.'

As she is silent, Gillian persists.

'His job must be waiting for him, isn't it?'

Robin stands in the doorway.

'I'm ready when you are.'

'Robin, thank you, but I'm talking to Chrissie. It's really important. As you seem to know. She has to find out what her husband is doing. What he wants now.'

'Actually, I think that's Chrissie's business. Whatever she wants to do is her business.' He speaks in a low, firm voice.

'In fact, what I want to do, right now, is to listen to Robin's music.'

'And then, perhaps, I will open the letter while you are here. Ok? Agreed?'

She goes into the hall, takes the brown envelope out of the drawer, lays it on the kitchen table. While Robin plays his tune in her sitting room, leaning over the keyboard, his long fingers marking out the melody, she sits back on the sofa and lets the notes cascade around her. Gillian sits tightly on an armchair, her body rigid with expectation. Chrissie smiles to both her friends in the room and is content to wait.